“So what you [illegible] is that you’re [illegible] for a husband?”

Taking hold of her hand, Lex passed his thumb softly, sensuously, over the back of it.

A nervous lump thickened Christina’s throat. They were walking on treacherous ground. “That’s right. Setting out to deliberately find a spouse is—well—”

“Unromantic?”

“Yes. Love doesn’t happen by design.”

“And you think love is an important ingredient for marriage?”

“It’s *the* essential ingredient.”

She watched his lips spread into a wide, seductive smile as she suddenly found his hands on her shoulders and his head lowering to hers. She mentally shouted a self-warning to turn her head, to step back and away from him. Yet her body refused to obey. Instead, she felt her chin lift, her lips part, and then the totally male taste of him shattered her senses.

Dear Reader,

Thank you for revisiting the Sandbur ranch with me!

Lex Saddler has always wanted to emulate his loyal father. But he can't make a wife and children happy when he has neither. He can't even fall in love! Or so he believes.

When Christina Logan, the private investigator hired to investigate Paul Saddler's mysterious death, arrives at the Sandbur, she is immediately struck with a sense of family—something she's never had. Her parents' tumultuous divorce and her mother's subsequent multiple marriages have made Christina long for a real home where love and responsibility go hand in hand. She's determined to have the real thing or nothing at all.

Even after our parents have long left us, they continue to touch our lives in the choices we make and the emotions we feel. Thankfully, Lex and Christina eventually realize the lessons they've learned from their parents are enough to bond their love for a lifetime.

I hope you enjoy Lex's tale. Please drop by again soon to find out what happens when Mac and Ripp go in search of their missing mother!

God Bless each trail you ride!

Stella Bagwell

STELLA BAGWELL

COWBOY TO THE RESCUE

SPECIAL EDITION®

Published by Silhouette Books

America's Publisher of Contemporary Romance

Recycling programs for this product may not exist in your area.

ISBN-13: 978-0-373-65429-1
ISBN-10: 0-373-65429-4

COWBOY TO THE RESCUE

This edition published by arrangement with Harlequin Books S.A.

Visit Silhouette Books at www.eHarlequin.com

Printed in U.S.A.

Books by Stella Bagwell

Silhouette Special Edition

Found: One Runaway Bride #1049
**Penny Parker's Pregnant!* #1258
White Dove's Promise #1478
†*Should Have Been Her Child* #1570
†*His Defender* #1582
†*Her Texas Ranger* #1622
†*A Baby on the Ranch* #1648
In a Texas Minute #1677
†*Redwing's Lady* #1695
†*From Here to Texas* #1700
†*Taming a Dark Horse* #1709
†*A South Texas Christmas* #1789
†*The Rancher's Request* #1802
†*The Best Catch in Texas* #1814
†*Having the Cowboy's Baby* #1828
Paging Dr. Right #1843
†*Her Texas Lawman* #1911
†*Hitched to the Horseman* #1923
†*The Christmas She Always Wanted* #1935
†*Cowboy to the Rescue* #1947

*Twins on the Doorstep
†Men of the West

Silhouette Books

The Fortunes of Texas
The Heiress and the Sheriff

Maitland Maternity
Just for Christmas

A Bouquet of Babies
*"Baby on Her Doorstep"

Midnight Clear
*"Twins under the Tree"

Going to the Chapel
"The Bride's Big Adventure"

STELLA BAGWELL

began writing romance novels more than twenty years ago. Now, more than sixty books later, she likens her job to childbirth. The pain is great, but the rewards are too sweet to measure.

Stella married her high school sweetheart thirty-seven years ago and now the two live on the Texas coast, where the climate is tropical and the lifestyle blessedly slow. When Stella isn't spinning out tales of love, she's usually working outdoors on their little ranch, 6 Pines, helping her husband care for a herd of very spoiled horses.

They have a son, Jason, who is a high school math teacher and athletic coach.

To my late parents, who are still guiding my footsteps.
I miss you both.

Chapter One

"Who the hell is that?"

Lex Saddler's drawled question was directed to no one in particular in the dusty cattle pen, but it was spoken loud enough for his cousin Matt to hear.

The other man followed Lex's gaze across the ranch yard to see Geraldine Saddler, the matriarch of the Sandbur ranch, approaching the corral fence. The surprise wasn't Lex's mother, an attractive woman in her mid-sixties with silver, bobbed hair, but the person by her side. The tall, young woman with long red hair, dressed in a short black skirt and delicate high heels, was definitely a stranger.

"I don't know," Matt murmured, "but if she gets any closer, she's going to get coated with dust."

Behind the two men, several cowboys were roping calves and stretching them out for the branding iron. The indignant little bulls and heifers were bawling in loud protest as the stench of burning hair and black dust filled the hot, muggy air.

Squatting near one of the downed calves, a cowboy called out, "Hey, Matt, better come look at this one. Looks like he has a loose horn."

Grinning at Lex, Matt inclined his head toward the rapidly approaching women. "You go meet the company. I've got more important things to do."

"Yeah, right," Lex muttered dryly, not bothering to slap at the dust on his denim shirt or brown leather chaps as he walked over to the fence.

"Lex, climb out of there, please," Geraldine called to him. "I want you to meet someone."

As he mounted the fence, then dropped to the other side, he could feel the redhead eyeing him closely. Normally, the idea that a woman was giving him a second glance would have pleased him. He made no pretensions about his love for the opposite sex. Women made his world go around, and he soaked up any attention they wanted to throw his way. But something about this particular female was making him feel just a tad self-conscious. Instead of batting her eyes with appreciation, she was giving him a cool stare. Wouldn't his tough cousin have a laugh about that? he thought wryly.

Shoving a black cowboy hat to the back of his head, he sauntered over to the two women. His mother began to make introductions, but Lex was too interested in their guest to pick up more than a word here and there.

Thick auburn hair clouded around her shoulders in glistening waves. Her pale skin, with its faint dotting of freckles, reminded him of cream sprinkled with nutmeg, and her blue eyes, of a late-summer storm cloud. Beneath a faintly tip-tilted nose, her lips were plush and pink, the moist sheen on them implying she'd just touched them with the tip of her tongue.

"Lex? Did you hear me? This is Ms. Logan. Christina Logan. The private investigator that has agreed to take our case."

His mother's words cut into his meandering thoughts, adding even more shock to his addled senses. This was the P.I.? And his mother might call it *our* case, but he viewed it as hers. Even though he'd agreed to help, this was totally his mother's doing.

"Uh—yes." He jerked off his leather glove and quickly offered his hand to the beauty standing in front of him. "My pleasure, Ms. Logan."

Instead of touching her palm weakly against his, the woman totally surprised him by curling her fingers firmly around his and giving his whole hand a strong shake.

"Nice to meet you, Mr. Saddler."

"Oh, don't call him 'Mr.,'" Geraldine quickly interjected. "You'll make his head even bigger than it already is. He's Lex to everyone. Even you. Isn't that right, son?"

Lex glanced at his mother, then smiled at Christina Logan. "I'd be pleased if you'd call me Lex. After all, I'm sure we'll be getting to know each other very well in the coming days."

Not if she could help it, Christina thought as she eyed the tough cowboy standing in front of her.

When Geraldine Saddler had approached her about taking on this case of her husband's death, she'd been very excited. The Sandbur reputation was known all over the state of Texas and beyond. Besides being rich and prominent, the families had the reputation of being fair dealers. Solving this case for the Saddlers was definitely going to put a feather in her cap.

However, when Geraldine had spoken of her son and the role he would be playing to help Christina with information, she'd expected Lex to be a businessman. The kind that sat behind a desk all day, giving orders over the phone. The kind that had soft hands and plenty of employees to make sure they stayed that way.

She'd never expected the rough, tough specimen of masculinity standing before her. He was tall. At least six foot three. And his body was the lean, wiry kind full of strength and stamina. Straight hair in myriad shades of blond covered his forehead and lent a boyish look to his rugged, thirty-something features. White teeth gleamed against his tanned face as his smile zeroed in directly on her.

Christina wanted to turn and run. Instead, she dropped his hand and drew in a long, much-needed breath.

"Then Lex it will be," she said as casually as she could. "And you must call me Christina."

"Will you be working here much longer?" Geraldine asked her son.

The man's dark green eyes swung away from Christina's face and over to his mother's.

"Yeah," he answered. "Probably till dark. Why?"

Geraldine rolled her eyes as though her son was growing slow-witted. "Cook is preparing a special supper in honor of Christina's arrival. I'd appreciate it if you weren't late."

"I'll try not to be," he assured her. "But I'm not going to leave everything with Matt." He smiled at Christina. "You understand, don't you?"

Christina understood that this man had probably been charming females with that smile from the moment he'd been born.

"Perfectly," she told him, then quickly softened the word

with a faint smile. After all, the man was to be admired for working at all when he clearly didn't have to. Add to that, it was obviously important to him to carry out his part of the work, instead of leaving it all to the other men. "And don't feel you have to make a special effort to hurry on my account. Your mother and I have plenty to talk over."

"Seven thirty, Lex," Geraldine warned. "After that, I'm telling Cook to throw yours out."

"Ouch!" he exclaimed, with a grimace. "All right. I'd like to eat tonight, so I'd better get back to work. See you later, Christina."

He pulled the brim of his hat down low on his forehead, then tipped it toward Christina in an outrageously gallant way before he climbed over the fence and jumped back into the dusty corral.

Sighing, Geraldine turned toward her. "I'm sorry if my son seems indifferent, Christina. But don't worry. He'll come around. I'll see to that." She closed a hand around Christina's elbow and urged her toward the big hacienda-style ranch house in the distance. "Let's get out of this dust and get you settled."

Two hours later, Christina stood in the upstairs bedroom she'd be occupying while on the ranch, peering out the window at the shadows rapidly spreading across the lawn below. From this view, she could see only portions of the massive ranch yard, with its numerous barns, sheds and corrals. The area where Lex Saddler had been working earlier was blocked from her view by the branches of a massive live oak tree.

And that was okay with her. She didn't need to be sneaking extra peeks at the man. Not when his image was still crowding her mind, refusing to leave her alone.

He had trouble written all over that sexy face, and she'd

not traveled all the way from San Antonio to this South Texas ranch to let a rakish cowboy—or any man, for that matter—distract her from her job. She'd learned the hard way that men like Lex had a habit of turning a woman's life upside down, then leaving her alone to pick up the pieces. Now that she'd gotten herself glued back together after Mike's betrayal, she had no intention of letting another man turn her head.

Her lips pursed with grim determination, she walked over to a long pine dresser and gazed at her image in the mirror. Geraldine had insisted that the family didn't "dress up" for evening meals, so Christina had chosen to wear a casual skirt with a ruffled hem, topped with a sleeveless cotton sweater in the same coral color as the skirt. Her aim was not to be overly dressed up, but to still look nice enough to show respect to her hosts.

She was brushing the loose ends of her hair when a knock sounded on the bedroom door. Laying the brush back on the dresser top, she went to answer it and was faintly surprised to see Lex Saddler standing on the other side of the threshold. Obviously, he and his men had gotten all the little dogies marked with the Sandbur brand.

"Good evening, Christina."

Christina couldn't help herself. Before she could stop it, her gaze was sliding over him, noting the clean jeans and brown ostrich boots, the blue-and-white pin-striped shirt tucked inside a lean waistband, the long sleeves rolled back against corded brown forearms. At the moment his hat was absent. It appeared he'd made an effort to slick the thick blond hair back from his forehead, but a couple of strands had slipped from the restriction and were now teasing a toffee brown eyebrow. A faint stubble of whiskers said he either didn't like shaving or had lacked the time to pick up a razor.

But the faint brown shadow did nothing to detract from the man's appearance. In fact, he was even more sensual and sexual than she'd first thought, and it irked her that the mere sight of him elevated the beat of her heart.

"Good evening," she said, returned his greeting, then, with a quick glance at her watch, asked, "Am I late?"

He smiled. "Not at all. Mother's on the front porch. We thought you might like to come down and have a drink before supper."

"Sounds nice," she agreed.

She shut the bedroom door behind her, and as they started down a wide hallway leading to the staircase landing, he linked his arm though hers, smooth and easy. Christina realized he was an old hand at escorting women.

"So, do you like your room?" he asked. "If you don't, there are several more you could try."

"The room is lovely," she told him, then tossed him a glance. "And so is your ranch."

His brows arched upward, and then he chuckled. "My kind of woman," he drawled. "I think we're going to get along just fine."

Christina wasn't ready to make such a prediction. Especially when he was giving off such flirtatious vibes. She was here for work and work only. She wanted to get along with this man, which would allow her to resolve the case quickly. If she had to keep fending him off at every turn, she was in for a long row to hoe.

At the bottom of the long staircase, they crossed a wide living room with Spanish-tile floors, brown leather furniture and several sculptures and paintings depicting the history of the century-plus-old ranch. It was not the formal type of sitting room she would have expected in the home of such a wealthy family. Instead of being a showcase, it had a lived-in look, which had instantly put her at ease.

After passing through a short foyer, Lex guided her onto a long concrete porch with huge potted succulents and wicker furniture grouped at intervals along the covered portico. Somewhere in the middle, Geraldine Saddler sat in a fan-backed chair, sipping from a frosty glass.

When she spotted Christina and her son, she smiled brightly.

"I see Lex found you ready to come down," she said to Christina. "Would you like a margarita or a glass of wine?"

"A margarita would be fine," Christina replied.

"I'll get it," Lex told her. "Just sit wherever you'd like." He released his hold on her arm and headed to a small table where Cook had organized glasses, a bucket of ice and several choices of drinks.

The moment Lex left her side, it felt as though the tornado that had been traveling beside her had now moved safely away. At least for the time being.

Drawing in a slow breath, she took a seat directly across from Geraldine and smoothed the hem of her skirt across her thigh. She'd hardly gotten herself settled when Lex returned with her drink.

"Thank you," she murmured quietly.

"My pleasure," he said as he took the seat next to her. "And be careful with that thing. Cook pours in a lethal amount of tequila. You might want to drink it slowly. Not everyone can handle liquor like my mother," he added teasingly.

Geraldine scowled at her son. "Lex! You'll have Christina thinking I'm a sot! I only have one or two of these in the evenings and sometimes none at all!"

"Yeah, but one or two of those things would kick my head right off my shoulders," replied Lex.

Although he spoke in a joking tone, Christina was inclined to believe he was being more or less truthful. The sip she'd taken from her own glass was like a cold jolt of lightning. Her father would love this, she thought wryly. But then, she had to give the man credit. He'd not touched alcohol in five years and was getting his life in order again.

Christina smiled at her hostess. "It's delicious."

She could feel more than see Lex watching her.

"So tell me about being a private investigator," he prompted. "Have you always done this sort of job?"

She turned her gaze on him, then wished she hadn't. He had such a raw sex appeal that each time she gazed squarely at his tanned face and beach-blond hair, she felt her stomach clench, her breath catch.

Stop it, Christina! You're not a teenager. You're a thirty-three-year-old woman who understands firsthand how a good-looking man can wreak havoc on a woman's common sense.

"No. I was twenty-two when I first went into law enforcement for the San Antonio Police Department. I remained on the force there for four years. Then I had an offer for an office position with the Texas Rangers. I worked there five more years before I finally decided I wanted to go into business for myself."

He casually crossed his ankles out in front of him, and from beneath her lowered lashes, Christina followed the long length of his legs with her eyes, all the way down to the square toes of his boots. If there was ever a complete description of a Texas cowboy, Lex Saddler was it.

"So what made you interested in law enforcement?" he asked. "Did you follow a relative into that profession?"

Christina might have laughed if the reality of her family situation hadn't been so sad. Her father had fought his own demons while trying to work in a family business that he'd had little or no interest in. And then there was her mother, who had flitted from one man to the next in hopes of finding happiness. No, her parents had lacked the dedication it took to work in law enforcement.

"None of my relatives have been in law enforcement of any sort. I just happened to find it interesting. I decided I wanted to spend my time helping folks find lost loved ones. Most of my cases consist of missing persons."

His brows arched slightly. "Well, my father is hardly missing, Christina. He's in the Sandbur cemetery. Along with the other family members that have passed on."

Her chin lifted a fraction. "I said I work *mostly* on missing-person cases, Lex. I didn't say I worked on those types of cases exclusively."

Geraldine eased forward in her chair. "Unfortunately, my daughters Nicci and Mercedes couldn't be here this evening. But they're agreeable to what I decide, and Lex has promised to keep them informed. They, like Lex, have had doubts about their father's death. But none of them wanted to voice them out loud."

He grimaced as though the whole subject was something he didn't want to ponder. "Well, hell, Mom, we've all had our doubts. But I want to believe the police. They concluded that a heart attack contributed to his drowning. The police and county coroner made a ruling. Why can't you accept their findings? What can Christina do that they've not already done?"

Geraldine swallowed down the last of her drink and set her glass aside. "I'll tell you what. She can look into all the weird things that were going on just before your father died."

Lex drew his feet back to him and sat up in his chair. "I

was living right here at home at the time, and I don't recall anything *that* weird going on. Dad was a little stressed out, but we all get like that at one time or another," he reasoned.

Geraldine sighed as she darted a glance at Christina, then her son. "Lex, when Paul's accident happened, I tried to tell you and your sisters that all had not been right with your father. Something was troubling him. I tried to get him to tell me what was going on, but he always gave me evasive replies and danced around my questions. That was totally out of character for Paul. I have no idea if his odd behavior had any connection to his death, but now with Wolfe wanting me to become a part of his life, I need to know what your father was doing and why. I don't want anything from the past to hurt Wolfe's chances for the future."

Lex was clearly disturbed by his mother's remarks, and for a moment, Christina expected him to jump to his feet and stalk off the porch. Instead, he thrust a frustrated hand through his hair.

"Surely you can't think that Dad was doing anything wrong!"

The older woman held her palms upward in a gesture that asked her son to understand. "Lex, I believe your father was an honest man until the day he died. But something was going on in his life that we didn't know about. That's why I've hired Christina. To figure it all out."

This seemed to trouble Lex even more, and he left his chair to pace back and forth in front of his mother. "Damn it, Mother, I understand that there are loose ends to Dad's life that you'd like to have explained. But I can't see the point in digging up something that is just downright painful. It won't bring Dad back. Nothing can. Now if you'll excuse me, I'm going to go see if Cook has supper ready."

Before Christina or Geraldine could say a word, he left the porch and entered the house.

With a weary sigh, Geraldine dropped her head in her hand. "I'm sorry, Christina. Before I hired you, Lex tried to dissuade me. He believes it's better to let sleeping dogs lie. But now that you're here…he'll accept my choice to find the truth. Just be patient with him."

Despite her calm demeanor, Christina could see that the woman was upset by her son's reluctant attitude.

Rising from her chair, Christina moved close enough to lay a reassuring hand on the matriarch's shoulder. "Don't worry, Geraldine. I'm sure your son is a reasonable person. He'll eventually understand that you and your whole family deserve to know the real truth of Paul's situation at the time of his death."

Smiling wanly, Geraldine nodded. "I'd better go have a talk with him. I want him to be sociable when he comes to the supper table. You might not believe it, but Lex is actually a very charming guy."

Oh, I believe it all right, Christina thought dryly. But he was clearly a strong-minded guy, too, and she wondered what it was going to take for Geraldine to draw him around to her way of thinking.

Patting Geraldine's shoulder, she said, "If you don't mind, I wish you'd let me talk to him. I think I know what he needs to hear, and it might be easier coming from an outsider instead of a relative."

With a grateful smile, Geraldine gestured toward the front door of the house, and Christina took off with a hurried stride. She wanted to find Mr. Cowboy before he had a chance to etch his mindset in stone.

Inside the house, Christina headed straight to the kitchen,

and even before she pushed through the swinging doors, she could hear his voice echoing off the low-beamed ceiling.

"—she's doing! It's a hell of a thing to see the mother I've always admired so wrapped up in a man that she can't see how she's upsetting the rest of the family! I—"

Not wanting to be an eavesdropper, Christina took a deep breath and pushed on into the room. Lex immediately heard the sound of her footsteps and whirled away from the tall, black-haired woman working at a huge gas range.

Surprised, he stepped toward her. "Are you looking for something?" he asked.

Giving him her best smile, Christina walked over to him. "Yes, I'm looking for you."

For one brief moment a sheepish look crossed his face, telling Christina that in spite of his quick exit from the porch, the man apparently possessed enough innate manners to be embarrassed at the way he'd behaved.

"I'm sorry I left the porch so abruptly, Christina, but I'm—not in the mood to discuss this thing about Dad right now."

Still smiling, she shrugged. "I think we should. Otherwise, none of us will enjoy our meal." She glanced over his shoulder at the woman standing at the range. Before she'd arrived at the Sandbur, Geraldine had told her a bit about Hattie, known to most everyone as simply Cook, including the fact that she was seventy-two and had worked on the ranch for nearly fifty years. Clearly, she was a part of the family, too, so Christina didn't see any reason not to speak freely in front of her. "And from the smell of this room, I can't wait to sample Cook's dishes."

Picking up on Christina's comment, Cook said, "This young lady has some common sense, Lex. Not like those tarts you associate yourself with. You'd better listen to this one."

Tossing Cook an annoyed glare, Lex reached for Christina's arm. "All right. Come along and we'll step out back."

On the opposite wall of the kitchen, they passed through a paned glass door and onto a large patio covered with an arbor of honeysuckle vines. The scent from the blossoms was heavenly, but Christina could hardly pause to enjoy it. After several long steps, Lex turned to face her.

"Okay, say what you feel you need to, and let's get this over with."

Refusing to allow his bluntness to get to her, she put on her most composed face.

"First of all, I've known your mother for only three weeks. But after the first conversation I had with her, it was obvious to me that she loved her late husband very much—that they had a very special relationship. If it took me only a few minutes to recognize that, I wonder why you can't see it after—" Her brows arched inquisitively. "What? Thirty-five years?"

"Good guess. But my age has nothing to do with this." Glancing away from her, he paused, then spoke again. "Listen, I'm not doubting my mother's love for my father. But now—well, I'm having a hell of a problem with these motives of hers. Especially the part about Wolfe Maddson." He planted a stare directly on her face. "The cause of my father's death should have nothing to do with their relationship, and I resent that she thinks it does."

The man wasn't annoyed, she realized; he was hurting. He believed his mother was betraying him and his father's memory. And Christina wasn't altogether sure that he was wrong. If she were in his shoes, she couldn't say she would be behaving any differently. But her job was not to judge, but to follow the wishes of her client.

"Look," she tried to reason, "it's important to your mother to have the truth—whatever that truth might be."

He moved closer and the scent of the masculine cologne clinging to his clothes mingled with the honeysuckle above their heads. She wondered if it was scientifically possible for scents to make a person drunk. What else could be making her feel so light-headed?

"Sure," he said wearily. "It's easy for you to stand there and make a pitch for Mom's plans. It's just business to you—you have no idea what it's like to lose someone as we did."

Christina kept reminding herself to keep this man's words impersonal. He couldn't possibly know that his comments were evoking tragic memories, whirling her back twelve long years ago, when she'd sat staring out a dark window, wondering why her little brother had not yet arrived home. At that time he'd been eighteen, and she'd wanted to believe he was at a party and enjoying it too much to leave his friends.

"So the truth of the matter isn't important to you?" she asked in an oddly hoarse voice.

She could feel his eyes traveling over her face.

"If you're going to give me the old truth-will-set-me-free speech, then please don't waste your time," he said, with faint sarcasm. "I know what the truth is."

"Well, I don't," she muttered, then turned on shaky legs and headed back toward the house.

Behind her, Lex stared at her retreating figure. Seeing her so upset had brought him up short. He'd never meant to hurt her and he desperately needed to make her understand that. Quickly he caught up to her as she was about to enter the house and gently placed a hand on her shoulder.

"Christina, what's the matter? You're the one who wanted to talk this out."

Her face was suddenly a picture of amazement, and Lex found himself mesmerized by the rich copper color of her hair, the dark blaze in her eyes and the moist purse of her lips.

"Talk, not yell," she shot back at him. "I'm your mother's guest, not your whipping boy."

Boy? With her cheeks flushed and her eyes blazing like that, there wasn't one tiny particle about her that was remotely boyish. In fact, he'd never seen so much sensuality bundled up in one female. And he'd never felt himself reacting so strongly. Then the meaning of her words sank in, and Lex found himself feeling faintly ashamed of his behavior. Maybe he had been out of line.

"If that's what you think I was doing, then I apologize. I was just trying to make you see that digging up the past seems fruitless to me. And even a little unhealthy. Dad is dead. Nothing will change that."

Without warning, she suddenly stepped closer. So close that he could smell her musky rose perfume, count the freckles on her upturned nose.

Her blue eyes challenged his. "You're probably thinking that I don't understand what you're feeling. But believe me, Lex, I do. Twelve years ago, my little brother disappeared without a trace. And since that time, every day I wish for the truth and someone—anyone—to help me find it."

Stunned by her revelation, his grip on her shoulder eased just enough for her to turn away from him. But before she could open the door and step inside, he caught her by the forearm.

"Wait, Christina. Please," he added softly.

Slowly, she turned back to him, and he was struck hard as he caught the watery shimmer in her blue eyes.

"I think we've both said enough," she said in a choked voice.

He grimaced ruefully. “No. I’m sorry, Christina. Really sorry.”

She bent her head and instinctively he gathered her to him in a gentle hug. “If I sounded callous a bit earlier, forgive me. I didn’t know you’d lost anyone. I mean, I didn’t stop to think—except about my own feelings.”

She pushed out a long breath, and he closed his eyes as it skittered warmly against the side of his neck.

“This—you and I—is going all wrong, Lex. Maybe my coming here—asking you to work with me—is asking too much of you,” she said. Then easing herself away from the circle of his arms, she opened the door and left him standing on the patio.

Chapter Two

By the time Lex gathered himself enough to go after her, Christina was already heading back to the front porch and his mother.

Fortunately, he caught the woman before she reached the foyer and, with a hand around her fragile wrist, led her stiff, unyielding body over to a chesterfield couch.

"No matter what you think of me at this moment," he said as he eased down beside her, "I can't allow you to go out there and tell Mom the two of us can't work together."

One copper-colored brow arched upward. "Give me one good reason not to," she requested.

"I don't want to hurt her. Not for any reason."

Approval flickered in her eyes, and Lex was surprised at how good the sight of it made him feel.

"I'm glad you're putting her feelings first," she said.

"I promise you, Christina," he said, "I always care about

my mother's feelings. I just...this whole thing about digging into Dad's death is hard for me. But I promise to help you in any way I can."

Her hand reached over and covered his, and Lex had the greatest urge to lift her fingers to his lips, to taste her smooth skin. But he didn't. He could already see that she was intelligent and strong-minded, not the sort of woman he could easily charm into a brief, pleasant beguilement.

"Thank you for that, Lex," she said quietly and started to rise.

Lex caught her by the hand, causing her gaze to lift to his. The direct connection jolted him in a way that felt totally odd. Being with Christina Logan was making him feel like a teenage virgin, which was a bit ridiculous. He'd made love to many attractive females before. There wasn't any reason for Christina to be raising his pulse rate just by looking him in the eye.

"Just a minute, Christina. I—" He passed his thumb along the back of her hand and momentarily savored the feel of her creamy skin. "I just wanted to say how sorry I am about your brother. I can't imagine what it must feel like—the not knowing about him."

She let out a heavy breath, and from the shadows that suddenly crossed her face, Lex could plainly see the emotional toll the tragedy had taken on her.

"The not knowing is the worst part," she admitted.

The need to help her, to ease her grief somehow, hit Lex in a totally unexpected way, and for a brief second, the feeling staggered him. "I'd like for you to tell me about him sometime," he invited.

"Sometime, I will." Smiling wanly, she pulled her hand away from his grasp and rose to her feet. "I think now we'd better join your mother before she begins to wonder where we've gotten off to."

* * *

The next morning Christina was sitting in a small office located on the west side of the house. Information regarding Paul Saddler's case was stacked on the floor in countless cardboard boxes and plastic storage containers. But at the moment she wasn't digging through any of it. Instead, she was on the phone to a friend.

Olivia Mills was a criminal lawyer, an associate of the San Antonio firm of Mills, Wagner & Murray. Several years ago, when Christina had stumbled onto some information that had proved a client of Olivia's innocent, the two women had become fast friends. And when Christina had decided to go into the private investigation business, Olivia had encouraged her to get an office in the same building as the firm's. As a result, Christina picked up many of the investigative jobs the firm often required.

"So tell me about the place," Olivia urged. "Is it anything like you expected?"

Christina settled back in the leather desk chair. "Not exactly. It's much larger than I imagined. If you drove forty miles in any direction you'd probably still be on Sandbur land. In fact, the ranch is organized into two divisions. The one with the house and working ranch yard, where I'm staying, is called the Goliad Division, and the western half of the property is the Mission River Division."

"Incredible. What's the house like?"

"Grandeur, but comfortable. It's a two-story hacienda and so large that I couldn't begin to count the number of rooms it has."

"Sounds like a lot of old money."

"It is. But these people are very unpretentious and laid-back, Ollie."

"That would be a relief for me."

Yes, it was a relief that the Saddlers weren't snobs. But maybe it would have been easier on her state of mind if Lex had been a snooty sort of person, she thought. Picking up a pencil, Christina began to doodle in a small open notebook. "So far they've treated me very nearly like family."

"Lucky dog," Olivia replied. "None of this sounds like work to me. I've always wanted to visit a big working ranch—just to see if those cowboys look as good in the rough as they do in pictures."

Christina bit back a sigh. She should be thanking God for this cushy job, which had virtually fallen into her lap, but this morning she wasn't at all convinced that she should be here. Not because she doubted her ability to find the cause of Paul's questionable death, but more because of the impact Lex Saddler was having upon her. She couldn't get the man out of her head.

"Believe me, Ollie, this case is not exactly simple. I'm going to have my work cut out for me."

"So you don't know how long you'll be staying on the ranch?"

She began to draw a horse, then a man wearing a pair of chaps. "No longer than necessary. I want to wrap this thing up as quickly as possible."

There was a long pause, and she could hear a frown in Olivia's voice when the other woman finally spoke.

"Is anything wrong? I've never heard you talk this way before. Normally, you're happily willing to invest whatever time it takes to wrap up a job."

Christina glanced at the open door to the office while wondering if any of the maids or family members might be within earshot. To be on the safe side, she lowered her voice to nearly a whisper. "Ollie, I'm just not comfortable here.

Ms. Saddler's son is not at all what I expected. In fact, he's been—quite a shock."

"Oh?" Olivia sounded intrigued. "What's wrong with the man?"

Christina pressed the fingertips of her right hand to her forehead. She'd hardly gotten four hours of sleep last night, and the lack of rest was already catching up to her. "If you don't count single, sexy and flirtatious as problems, then he's okay. I thought he was going to be a businessman, Ollie. And he is—but he's not exactly the desk sort. He's a cowboy. He wears boots and spurs and gets sweaty and dusty just like the other cowhands."

Olivia chuckled. "My, oh my, that sounds like a handful of assets to me."

Christina rolled her eyes. "You would think so. But I'm trying to keep my mind on business."

The other woman let out a disapproving groan. "You *always* have business on your mind. Maybe this—what's his name?"

Christina smiled in spite of herself. "Lex. His name is Lex Saddler."

"Maybe this Lex will remind you that you're a young, beautiful woman ready for a new man in your life."

Christina didn't know if she'd ever be ready for another man, but she wasn't going to waste time rehashing the old argument with her dear friend.

"I've got a ton of work to get started on, Ollie. I'll see you later in the week. I think I've got a handle on your missing witness, so I might be able to give you his definite whereabouts then."

"Great. We'll talk more when you get back to the city. But before you hang up just remember this—Mr. Lex Saddler isn't a police officer."

Christina grimaced. Olivia ought to know there wasn't any need for her to bring up good-time, no-commitment Mike. A woman didn't ever forget a mistake like him.

"As if that makes any difference," Christina said dryly, then quickly told her friend goodbye and folded the cell phone together.

In the back of the house, Lex was in the kitchen, dancing Cook across the tiled floor as an old country song played on the radio.

"What are you doing here in the kitchen again?" Cook, demanded. "You've already had your breakfast. You should be down at the cattle pens."

He twirled the aging but agile woman beneath his arm. "Yeah, I should be. Matt had to pull Lester off the fence building crew to take up my slack 'cause I've got other duties this morning," he said with a grimace. "I've told Mom that I don't want her fretting over Dad's case, so I'm going to be dealing with it and Ms. Logan. And this morning, she needs my assistance."

Cook's sly smile spread her ruby-red lips. "Ms. Logan, eh? Well, that ought to make you a happy man. So why aren't you smilin', and why are you wastin' time in here with me?"

He grinned. "What man wouldn't want to start out his day dancing with his sweetheart?"

She snorted. "I've known plenty."

Lex chuckled. "Then they weren't worth knowing."

Cook pinched his shoulder. "Be serious and talk to me."

Her order came just as the song ended, so he led the woman over to a long pine table bracketed with benches made of the same wood. After she was seated, he poured two cups of coffee and carried them over to the table.

"I'm not going to beat around the bush, Hattie, I'll come right out and say that I think Mom has slipped a cog. Or that damned senator has brainwashed her!"

Clearly disgusted with his analogy, she said, "What are you talkin' about? Geraldine is as sharp as a tack."

He eased down next to her. "Hattie, when she first talked to me about hiring a private investigator, I wasn't wild about digging into Dad's death. But I could see the whole thing was important to her, so I went along with her wishes. If Dad's death wasn't an accident, then we need to know it. But last night…well, I got the impression from Mom that she's doing all of this just to prove to Wolfe Maddson that the Saddler family doesn't have any hidden skeletons that could come out and hurt his political career. I'll tell you one thing, Hattie. If that man thinks my mother has to present a clean background to him before he'll walk down the aisle with her, then he's gonna be knocked on his ass, and I'm going to be the one doing the knocking!"

Impatient with his attitude, Cook merely looked at him and shook her head. "So what if that's Geraldine's motive? You can use this opportunity to prove to Wolfe Maddson that your father was the honorable man everyone believed him to be. It'll make the man see that if he plans to keep your mother as happy as Paul did, then he's got big, big boots to fill." Her features softened as she laid a hand on his shoulder. "Besides, it won't be no skin off your hide to work with a pretty thing like Ms. Logan. She seems awfully sweet to me."

A wry grin spread slowly across Lex's face. "Yeah. But you've always told me that too many sweets were bad for my health."

Patting his cheek, she gave him a wink. "Yes, but that's the thing about you, boy. You like being bad."

Five minutes later, as Lex walked out of the kitchen and headed to Christina's temporary office, he thought about Cook's comment. Like the rest of his friends and family, she considered him a ladies' man, a guy who worked hard but played even harder. None of them understood that most of his flirtatious behavior was just a cover, that his frequent dates were only attempts to fill the lonely holes inside him.

Both his sisters were married now. Nicci, the oldest, had a new daughter, and Mercedes, his younger sister, had announced a few weeks ago that she and her husband, Gabe, were expecting their first child. All three of his cousins also had loving spouses and growing families. Lex was the only unmarried relative left in the Saddler and Sanchez bunch, unless he counted Cook, his mother and his uncle Mingo. But who knew? By the end of the year, even the old folks would probably have lifelong partners.

What are you whining about, Lex? If you wanted to be married that badly, you wouldn't be so particular. You'd settle for a woman you liked, a woman who'd be a good wife, instead of waiting for that one precious love to come along and wham you in the heart.

Pushing those pestering notions out of his head, Lex knocked lightly on the open door, then stepped into the room.

Christina was sitting behind a large oak desk, black-rimmed reading glasses perched on the end of her nose as she studied a paper filled with typed text.

Lifting her head, she smiled at him. "Good morning."

"Good morning, yourself." Moving over to the desk, he leaned a hip against the edge. "Cook tells me you've already had breakfast."

She glanced at a small silver watch on her left wrist. "About an hour ago. What about you?"

He smiled with amusement. "About three hours ago."

Laying the paper aside, she leaned back in her chair. Lex couldn't prevent his eyes from drinking their fill. She was dressed casually this morning in an aqua-colored shirt and a pair of jeans. Her fiery hair was pulled into a ponytail, which made her look more like twenty-three than thirty-three, the age his mother had disclosed about the private investigator.

"You must be an early riser," she commented.

"It's a rancher's necessity," he told her. "If he plans to get things done."

She smiled wanly. "And I'm going to assume that you're a man who gets things done."

Was she making fun of him? It didn't matter. She was a city girl. She didn't know about his sort of life. Or him.

"When I try," he drawled. He pointed to the paper she'd been reading. "Is that something about my father's case?"

She nodded. "It is. But it's nothing from your father's personal things. I've not started going through them yet. Before I drove down from San Antonio, I gathered some general information about the company he worked for—Coastal Oil. It's a huge conglomerate now. They've expanded several times during the past few years."

The button just above her breasts had been left undone, and if he angled his head just right, Lex could see a tiny silver cross dangling in the shadowed cleavage. Strangely, the sight was both erotic and prim. Like a good girl hiding a naughty tattoo.

"I don't know of any oil company nowadays that isn't making a killing. Yet that wasn't quite true eleven years ago. Coastal Oil was close to going bankrupt."

Her expression thoughtful, she said, "The economy ebbs and flows on cyclical tides. Could be that was simply a downtime for raw crude. Or perhaps the problem was poor management."

"Yeah. Or corrupt management," Lex replied.

Her brows arched. "Why would you make a remark like that? Do you know for a fact that someone was stealing from the company?"

"Not at all. I was just speculating. Nowadays white-collar crime seems to be rampant."

The curiosity that had been marking her face swiftly disappeared. "That's true."

Feeling restless now, Lex walked over to a window that looked out upon the ranch yard. At the moment, he could see Gabe, the Sandbur's horse trainer, down at the horse pen, riding a red roan filly. The animal was trying to get her head low enough to buck, but the man was doing his best to change her mind. His brother-in-law was a genius with horses. And women, too, apparently. He'd certainly made Lex's sister Mercedes happy.

Lex glanced over his shoulder at Christina. She'd removed the glasses from her face and was eyeing him with easy anticipation. Just to look at her, Lex found it hard to imagine her working on a police force, putting herself in dangerous situations.

"What makes you do what you do?" he asked.

"My brother. When he disappeared, the police were useless—or so it seemed. I truly believed that I could do better. Later, after I finally learned how things really worked on the police force, I could see that finding a missing person wasn't as simple as I'd first imagined." She leaned forward and folded her hands together on the desk top. "Working with the Rangers was more than great—it was the chance of a lifetime to garner the experience I needed."

"Why didn't you stay there?"

One slender shoulder lifted and fell. "Because I didn't want to spend the rest of my life sitting behind a desk."

Lex gestured toward her. "Looks like you're still sitting behind one."

She appeared faintly amused as she rose to her feet and walked over to a wall lined with book-filled shelves. Lex hoped she stayed there. If she drew near him, he'd be able to smell her rose-scented perfume. He'd want to look at places he shouldn't and touch even more. He'd find it damned hard to remain a gentleman.

"But you see, I can get up whenever I want," she pointed out. "I don't have a superior telling me what to do or how to go about doing it. If I need to bend the rules a bit, I can take that risk, because I'm the only one who might get hurt."

Where was all her confidence coming from? Lex wondered. Or was it more like determination? The question lingered in his mind as his gaze wandered discreetly down her slender curves. Most of the women he'd dated were attractive, but none of them were nearly as interesting as Christina. He realized there were many things he'd like to ask her, but they were all so personal, he decided he'd better keep the questions to himself. At least, for a while.

"You obviously like being your own boss," he stated.

She glanced at him and smiled, and Lex felt a spurt of desire as he watched her pink lips spread against very white teeth. She was like a field of spring wildflowers. A man couldn't ignore all that vibrant color.

"Don't you?" she countered.

Her assumption made him chuckle. "If you think I'm the boss around here, you're mistaken. Matt Sanchez, my cousin, is the general manager, but even he doesn't consider himself the head cheese of the Sandbur. No one does. We're family, and we work as a unit—makes us stronger that way."

His words sent an odd little pain through Christina's chest. To be a part of a family, and to have that family whole and strongly webbed together with love, was all that she'd ever wanted. But her parents had never known or learned how to love themselves, much less each other or their children, as deeply as they should have. They'd split apart when she and Joel had been young teenagers. Then to add to that messy wound, Joel had gone missing, ripping away what little family she'd had left.

To hide her dark, unsettled thoughts, she quickly pretended an interest in the books in front of her. "Anything whole is always stronger than something divided." She darted a glance at him. "You're a lucky man, Lex Saddler."

He didn't say anything to that, and though her head was turned away from him, she could feel his thoughtful silence, his warm gaze traveling over her.

"So where do you plan to start this morning on Dad's case?"

Bracing herself, she turned to face him. "Right now I have copies of the police and coroner's reports, so-called witness depositions and general information about the company Paul worked for. Your mother has given me pertinent data as to where Paul grew up, how they met and a general idea of their marriage, especially around the time that he died. For the next couple of days, I'm going to delve into all that."

"So what do you need from me? I mean this morning."

No doubt he was itching to get outside, and she couldn't blame the man. From the few open spaces between the live oak limbs shading the window, sunshine was streaming through the panes of glass, slanting golden stripes across the hardwood floor. Out on the lawn, dew glistened on the thick

Saint Augustine grass while mockingbirds squawked angrily at a pair of fox squirrels. It was a lovely morning. One that needed to be taken advantage of.

She looked at Lex speculatively. He was a man who needed to be doing. Sitting and talking about the past would only make him tense again.

Smiling tentatively, she walked toward him. "I'd like for you to take me on a horseback ride."

Chapter Three

Like an idiot, Lex felt his jaw drop as he stared at the lovely woman in front of him. He'd been expecting a taped question-and-answer session or, at the very least, to help her go over stacks of his father's personal papers.

"Riding? For pleasure?"

She laughed softly. "Why, yes. That's the only sort of riding I've ever done. Don't you ever ride across the hills just for the sake of riding?"

He stroked a thumb and forefinger against his chin. "Not since I was about ten years old. After that, I got on a horse to go someplace or to herd cattle. And as for hills, the only kind we have around here are fire-ant hills."

Dimples appeared in both her cheeks, and Lex felt the middle of his chest go soft and gooey. What was the matter with him? he wondered. A woman's simple smile had never affected him this way.

"Well, perhaps this morning you could pretend you're herding cattle, and we could talk a bit about your father's case along the way? It's a shame to waste the sunshine, and I'd enjoy seeing some of the ranch."

She was making spending time with her easy, Lex thought, way too easy.

"Then you've got a date." He glanced at her strapped sandals. "Do you own a pair of boots? Not the kind you wear down a fashion runway, either. The cowboy kind that will hold your feet in the stirrups?"

"I do. Give me five minutes to change. Where shall I meet you?" she asked.

"In the kitchen. Cook will give us some cookies and a thermos of coffee to take."

"I thought you didn't know how to ride for fun," she reminded him.

Feeling unexpectedly happy, he laughed. "I'm a quick learner."

Ten minutes later, the two of them were out the door and walking toward an enormous white wooden barn. At the nearest end, and along one side, wooden corrals separated groups of horses, some of which were munching alfalfa hay from portable mangers.

Inside the barn, Lex saddled a gentle mare named Hannah for Christina and, for himself, a paint gelding called Leo that he most often used as a working mount.

While he readied the horses, Christina used the time to look around the inside of the cavernous barn. Besides the outside horses, there were at least thirty stalled inside the structure, and though she was far from an expert on horse flesh, she recognized without being told that some of the animals were worth a small fortune. Their stalls were pristine, and their coats, manes and tails groomed to perfection.

A number of wranglers and stable boys were already hard at work, and she could easily see why the Sandbur was one of the largest and wealthiest ranches in the state of Texas. But whether that wealth had played into Paul Saddler's death was yet to be seen.

"We'll take them outside and mount up there," Lex told her. "Can you lead Hannah?"

"Sure. I'm not a complete greenhorn around horses." He handed Hannah's reins to her, and as they headed toward the open barn door, the gray mare fell into obedient step behind her. "One of my best childhood friends owns horses and keeps them stabled at the edge of the city. We've ridden together since we were small girls," she told him. "Only lately, I've gotten out of practice. She has to fly back and forth to California to care for her ailing mother."

He glanced over at her. "That must be stressful. What about your mother? Does she live in San Antonio?"

Christina caught herself before she grimaced. Frowning at the mention of her mother wouldn't make a good impression. Especially to someone like Lex, who obviously adored his mother. But he could hardly know the sort of life that Retha Logan had lived. He couldn't know that in her fifty-one years of life, she'd already gone through six husbands and was now working on her seventh.

"No, she lives in Dallas."

"You see her often?"

"Not too often. She stays busy, and so do I."

"What about your father?"

His questions were simple and something to be expected. Even so, they made her feel very uncomfortable. Especially when she was the one who usually did the asking, not the answering.

"He still lives in San Antonio," she conceded. "You see, my parents divorced when my brother and I were teenagers. So it's been a long time since we were all together as a family."

"Oh. Sorry."

Thankfully, they'd reached the open yard in front of the horse barn, and Christina halted her forward motion. "Can we mount up now?"

"I'm ready," he agreed, allowing Leo's reins to dangle to the ground and turning toward her. "Let me help you."

"Won't your horse run off?" she asked, with dismay.

"No. He understands what I want him to do."

"Smart horse."

He chuckled. "That's the only kind we raise here on the Sandbur."

Christina stood to one side as he slipped the bridle reins over Hannah's head.

"Put your foot in the stirrup, and I'll give you a boost," he said.

His boost turned out to be a hand on her rump, pushing her upward, but when she landed in the seat of the saddle with hardly any effort at all on her part, she couldn't be cross with him.

As he swung himself onto the back of the paint, she said, "I suppose that's a technique you use to help everyone into the saddle."

He laughed under his breath, and Christina realized she'd never heard a more sexy sound.

"Well, just the women. None of the men around here need help getting into the saddle."

Women. No doubt he had girlfriends in the plural, she

thought. He had that rakish, devil-may-care attitude that drew women like bears to a beehive. She ought to know. Mike had been a charmer deluxe, the smoothest-talking man she'd ever run across. Still, that shouldn't have been any excuse for her to go on believing his gaff for four long years. Once she'd finally smartened up and left, she'd vowed to never believe anything a smooth-talking man said without some sort of action to back it up.

Lex nudged his horse forward, and Christina quickly drew the mare abreast of Leo. As they moved away from the barn, he pointed in a westerly direction.

"The river is that way, and that's where my sisters love to ride," he said. "But the trail is rough. We'll go north today and travel the road that leads to the vet's house. Maybe later, after I see how well you can ride, we'll go to the river one day."

Christina had only suggested getting out this morning because she'd believed it would be a way of getting Lex to relax and talk more freely about his father. She'd not been thinking about future days or spending any more casual time with this man. But now that they were riding along, their stirrups brushing, the wind at their back and a crooked, contagious grin on Lex's face, she could very easily imagine doing all this again. It was a dangerous thought…especially since it seemed so tempting.

"I promise not to hurt Hannah or myself," she assured him.

Forty minutes later, they reached a small stream with a low wooden bridge. On the other side of the little creek was a small house shaded by oaks, a barn and a network of cattle pens. Before they crossed the bridge, Lex suggested they stop for a break. After dismounting, he tethered their horses to a nearby willow tree and pulled the thermos of coffee and plastic-wrapped cookies from his saddle bags.

"Is that the vet's house?" Christina asked as they took seats on the side of the bridge.

"Yeah, Jubal and his family live there. He's our resident veterinarian. I don't think any of them are home at the moment, but I'm sure you'll get a chance to meet them all later. Angie has a teaching degree, but for now she's staying home to take care of their daughter, Melanie, and baby son, Daniel."

Another real family, Christina thought wistfully. The Sandbur seemed to be full of them, reminding her just how unsuccessful she'd been in finding a man to love her and give her children.

"Sounds like a nice family."

"They are," he agreed, then handed her the bag of cookies. "Here. I'd better warn you that you can't eat only one. They're too good."

After a breakfast of eggs and biscuits, she wasn't the least bit hungry, but after one bite of pecans and chocolate chips, she couldn't resist eating a whole cookie and wistfully eyeing those that remained.

He took a short drink from the thermos cup, then passed it to her. For some reason, drinking after the man felt very intimate. As Christina sipped the hot liquid, she felt her cheeks grow unaccustomedly warm.

"So your father was a rancher, too," she commented after a few moments of easy silence had passed.

He picked up a tiny piece of gravel and tossed it into the shallow water. "For most of his early life—before he went to work in the oil business. And even after that, he helped here on the ranch as much as time allowed. Even to this day, I don't know half as much about cattle as he did. He was a very intelligent man."

There was love and pride in his voice, and Christina

wondered how it would feel, to know her father had lived an admirable life. She was very proud that Delbert Logan was now staying sober, holding down a good job and taking care of himself, instead of expecting someone to take care of him. Still, she couldn't help but envy the relationship Lex had clearly had with his father.

"That's what I keep hearing." She smiled at him. "It's obvious that you were very close to him. Did he spend much time with all his children?"

"As much as possible. My sisters were very close to our father, too. But whenever he was home on the ranch, he and I were practically inseparable."

"So you were living here on the ranch at the time of his death?"

He nodded grimly. "I hadn't been out of college long and had moved back home from Texas A&M. God, I'm just thankful he got to see me graduate."

No doubt, Paul Saddler would be proud of his son if he could see him now, Christina thought. Lex appeared to be a man who loved his family deeply and was dedicated to doing his part to keep their ranch successful.

"So what made your father decide to go into the oil business, anyway?"

Lex shrugged. "I'm not exactly sure. I was still in grade school when that happened. I think it was a time when cattle prices had sunk to the bottom of the barrel, and Dad decided he'd be more help to the ranch if he brought in outside money. You see, he'd graduated college with a chemical engineering degree and had always planned to work for one of the chemical plants located on the coast. But then he met my mother, and after they married, he decided that ranching would make him just as happy."

"Hmm. So he went to work at Coastal Oil out of necessity?" she asked.

Lex nodded. "But I think after he'd been with the company awhile, the money and the benefits became too good to leave. Plus, he was getting something out of his degree. And then there was always the thought of a nice retirement check, which gave him more incentive to stay."

She handed the thermos cup back to him. "Did you personally know the three friends Paul worked with? The ones who were with him the day of his accident?"

He poured more coffee into the metal cup. "Yes. They seemed to be okay guys, I suppose. Mom has always loved to throw parties for a variety of reasons, and these guys would always attend—until Dad died. After that, they never came back to the ranch. Guess they thought it might bring up bad memories for Mom or something. I thought it was a bit odd, myself." He looked thoughtfully over at her. "Have you read through their testimonies?"

She nodded. "Yes, but I'm not putting too much stock in them. Most eyewitnesses are very unreliable. They don't accurately recall what happened, even though they swear they're sure about what they saw. And the ones that seem to remember every tiny detail are usually lying."

"Oh. Do you think Dad's friends accurately described what happened that day?"

"I don't yet know enough about them or the case to form an opinion." She gave him an encouraging smile. "Can you tell me more about them?"

His expression thoughtful, he gazed out at the open range dotted with gray Brahman cattle. "They were Dad's work buddies, not necessarily friends of mine. But I recall a little about them. Red Winters was a big, burly guy. A bit obnoxious, always telling crude jokes. He thought he knew more than everybody, including my dad. Which was a joke. Red got his job because of who he knew, not what he knew. Harve Dirksen was sort of the ladies' man type. Tall, dark, good-looking, and he knew it. About a year before Dad died, he was going through a messy divorce. I guess Mrs. Dirksen had gotten tired of his cheating. But in spite of their personal problems, they were always devoted friends to Dad. If he needed their help for any reason, they'd be there for him."

"What about the third man, Lawrence Carter?"

"The epitome of a nerd. Physically weak. Smart at his job, but socially backwards. He'd always been big in playing the stock market and had a degree in business along with being a chemist. Like I said, he was smart, but Red always bullied him around. I remember Mom mentioning that Lawrence had a sickly son, but I don't know what came of that. You might ask her about it. But I'm pretty sure his wife left him, too, sometime after Dad died. But his luck turned around eventually. All three men came into a small fortune about a year after Dad died."

Christina looked at him sharply. "Oh? How did that happen?"

Lex shrugged. "Dumping a bunch of company stock right before the value crashed. Just good timing, I suppose. A lot of stockholders lost all their retirement investments. Some demanded an investigation, but nothing criminal was ever proved."

The wheels inside Christina's head were clicking at a fast rate, but she didn't voice her thoughts aloud. She needed much more time and information before she could share with Lex any of the ideas she was entertaining. Instead, she said, "Well, could be the men were just savvy traders. Sometimes it's hard to tell a good businessman from a thief."

"Yeah." He rose from his perch on the bridge and offered a hand down to her. "We'd better be getting along. If you're ready, I'll show you the family cemetery before we head back to the ranch. It's a little west of here, but not too far."

"I'd like that."

She closed her fingers around his, and with no effort at all, he tugged her to her feet. The sudden momentum tilted her forward, and she instinctively threw her hands out to prevent herself from falling straight into his arms. They landed smack in the middle of his chest, and she found her face only inches from his.

"Oh! I—I'm sorry!" she said breathlessly. "I lost my balance."

As she started to push herself away, she realized that he had a steadying hold on both her arms.

"No need to apologize," he said, with a grin. "I'm just glad you didn't teeter over into the creek. You would have probably taken me with you."

She desperately wished he would release his hold on her. Standing this close to him was creating an earthquake in the pit of her stomach. Everything about him smelled like a man, felt like a man. And everything inside of her was reacting like a woman.

"That wouldn't have been any fun," she said, trying to keep her voice light.

"Oh, I don't know. Might be pleasant to have a little morning swim together."

The suggestive drawl of his voice clanged warning bells in the back of her head, and she quickly jerked away from the clasp of his hands. "I—uh, we better head on to the cemetery."

Christina walked off the bridge, and as she rapidly headed

toward the waiting horses, she sensed him following closely behind her.

Once she reached Hannah's side, the touch of his hand on the back of her shoulder drew her head around. As she met his gaze, she felt her breath lodging in her throat.

"Christina, are you okay?"

The softly spoken question caught her off guard, and for a moment she wasn't sure how to answer. "Why, yes. Why wouldn't I be?"

His brows pulled together in a frown of confusion. "Because I saw something on your face back there. You looked at me like you were scared and wanted to run away." He gently touched his fingertips to her cheek. "You're not frightened of me, are you?"

Totally disconcerted, she looked at the leather stirrup dangling near her waist, the ground where one of Hannah's hooves was stomping at a pestering fly, at anything and everything but him. "That's silly. Of course I'm not afraid of you."

Her heartbeat hammered out of control as he moved closer and his hand slid lightly up and down the side of her arm. "You don't need to worry about me, Christina. I would never hurt you or any woman."

No. She figured this man would die before he'd ever lay an angry hand on a woman. But there were countless ways to cause another person pain, and she wondered how many women in his past had cried themselves to sleep at night, waiting for a call, waiting to hear him say, "Honey, let's spend the rest of our lives together". She'd experienced firsthand some of the ways a man could hurt a woman, and she wasn't up to getting another dose of education on the subject.

Forcing a teasing smile to her face, she lifted her head and met his gaze. "The only thing I'm worried about is convincing your mother that I don't need you hanging at my side eight hours of the day."

That obviously surprised him. "You don't?"

"No. I always work alone. It's better for my concentration that way. If I come across things I need to ask you, I'll make notes and get to you later."

The relief on his face was almost insulting.

"Well, I do have plenty of work that can't be done by anyone else but me," he admitted. "And anyway, I'm not very good at putting puzzle pieces together. Now my sister Mercedes is a different matter. She worked as an intelligence gatherer for the military."

Christina nodded. "Yes. Geraldine told me. But she's pregnant with her first child, and Geraldine doesn't want to put any undue stress on her—especially with such dark matters. And your other sister, Nicci, has her days packed full with being a doctor and caring for her family. And your mother is incredibly busy, too. So that leaves you. But I don't expect you to drop everything and alter your life just because I'm here."

His gaze was almost suspicious as it roamed her face. "Are you giving me this reprieve for other reasons?"

Forcing a light chuckle, she turned her back to him and reached to untie Hannah's reins. "Reprieve? You make it sound like spending prolonged time with me would be a prison sentence."

"That's a ridiculous notion. You must realize that you're a very attractive woman. I'm sure you've never had a man complain about spending time with you."

No, she thought dismally. Mike had never complained

about spending time with her. Especially while they'd been making love. He'd just never wanted to make their time together into something permanent.

Glancing over her shoulder at him, she said, "You'd better get to know me before you say that."

"I plan to," he promised. Then reaching for her arm, he helped her back into the saddle.

During the next week Christina rarely saw Geraldine Saddler. The ranching matriarch was an extremely busy woman, spending most of her waking hours working on some sort of charity project or overseeing the actual running of the ranch's daily activities. It was as common to see her dressed in jeans and chaps, driving around in her old Ford truck, as it was to glimpse her leaving for San Antonio in a sequin and satin cocktail dress. She was a woman to be admired, and Christina envied her children for having such a strong, respected mother, a mother who viewed loving a man and raising his children as the most ultimate blessings and responsibilities in her life.

As for Lex, she'd been meeting with him in the evenings, after supper, to go over details of the investigation. So far she couldn't have asked for him to be a more perfect gentleman. And he'd even helped her begin to see inside the person who'd died in the gulf waters off Corpus Christi. She had to admit that Lex wasn't the problem that she'd first expected him to be. But her reaction to him was definitely a problem. A huge one.

She'd hoped that the more she was around the man, the more she'd be able to control her racing heart and quell the ridiculous heat that colored her cheeks and warmed every inch of her body whenever she was near him. Trouble was, the more she tried to fight the attraction she had for the rawhide-tough rancher, the stronger it seemed to grow.

That fact hit harder than ever later that evening, as she left her room to go to dinner. Halfway down the staircase, she met Lex coming up. He was dressed very casually in jeans and a short-sleeved polo shirt. The moss-green color set off the tawny-blond streaks in his hair and the dark tan of his arms. She drank in the sight of him like a parched flower soaking up raindrops.

"There you are," he said, with an easy smile. "I was just coming up to fetch you."

"Oh. Have you been waiting?"

"No. Mom is away for the evening, and I wanted to see if it was okay with you if we had our meal in the kitchen. I hope you're going to say yes, because I've already sent Cook home."

"Of course it's okay with me." In fact, Christina was happy about the change. Even though the dining room of the Saddler hacienda was very beautiful, she preferred a smaller, cozier setting to eat her meals, especially when there were only two people present.

"Good." He wrapped an arm through hers and began to escort her down the remaining stairs and in the general direction of the kitchen. "Would you like a drink first? Since Mom's not here, Cook didn't make margaritas, but I can shake something up."

Just the scent of him, the touch of his hand and the smile on his face were shaking her up. Much more than a splash of tequila. She wondered what he would think if he knew that. "Actually, I don't normally drink anything alcoholic."

He glanced her way. "If having it around bothers you, you should have told us."

Shaking her head, she said, "I don't expect people around me to be prudes, and I even drink spirits occasionally—you saw me drink a margarita the first evening I was here. But my father is a recovering alcoholic. Each time I take a sip, I think of what he's gone through."

"Oh, I'm sorry. How is your father doing now?"

She gave him a tentative smile. Talking honestly about Delbert Logan was something new for her. As a young girl, she'd often lied to her friends so they wouldn't know about her father's condition. Later on, as she'd grown into womanhood, she'd avoided talking about him altogether. Now, she sometimes had to remind herself that her father was becoming a different person. For the first time in her life, she could speak proudly of him. "He's not had a drink in over five years, and he's working at a good job. I never thought he'd find the determination to turn his life around, but he has. And that makes me very happy."

By now they were in a hallway that led to the kitchen, and when he paused and turned to her, she was suddenly reminded that the two of them were entirely alone in the big house.

"I'm glad for you, Christina," he said, with a gentle smile. "And I apologize if I was prying. You didn't have to tell me all that about your father. You could have told me to mind my own business."

The idea that he understood how difficult it was for her to talk about her father's problem suddenly made it all very easy, and she gave his arm a grateful squeeze.

"It's all right," she quietly assured him. "It's nice to be able to say good things about my father. I only wish my mother could get herself on a better track."

"What does that mean?"

She urged him to keep walking toward the kitchen, and

as the two of them strolled along, she said, "It means that my mother is nothing like yours. She's been married six times. Who knows? The next time I call her, it might be seven."

"Whew! And I was concerned about Mom marrying a second time."

She sighed. "Your mother is a steadfast saint compared to mine."

"What's up with your mother and all the marriages?"

Christina shrugged. "She's looking for something to make her happy," she said wearily. "Unfortunately, she believes she'll find it in a man."

"Ouch. You sound very cynical. Do I need to apologize for being male?" he teased.

She tried to laugh. "No. Just never compare me to my mother. I'm not a man hunter."

"That's not true," he countered as they reached the swinging doors of the kitchen.

Halting in her tracks, she turned an offended frown on him. "I beg your pardon?"

"You are hunting a man," he explained. "Your brother."

She visibly relaxed. "Oh. Yes. But that's different."

Taking hold of her hand, he passed his thumb softly, sensuously over the back of it. "So what you're trying to tell me is that you're not looking for a husband?"

Her head bobbed jerkily up and down as a nervous lump thickened her throat. They were walking on treacherous ground, and the fact that there was no one around to interrupt them made her even more wary. "That's right. Setting out to deliberately find a spouse is…well—"

"Unromantic?"

"Yes. Love doesn't happen by design."

The dimples in his cheeks made Christina wonder if he

was finding her attitude very amusing, or if he was simply enjoying this intimate exchange with her. Either way, her heart was fluttering so madly, she wondered what was keeping her from fainting.

"And you think *love* is an important ingredient for marriage?" he asked.

Just hearing him say the word "love" was enough to steal Christina's breath. Which made her feel like even more of an idiot for reacting so strongly to this man. "It's *the* essential ingredient. Now, do you think we can go in to our supper? This conversation is ridiculous."

His smile slowly turned suggestive. "The conversation might be senseless, but this isn't."

Christina was trying to make sense of his words when she suddenly found his hands on her shoulders and his head lowering to hers. Stunned by the idea that he was about to kiss her, she mentally shouted a warning to herself to turn her head, to step back and away from him. Yet her body refused to obey the signals of her brain. Instead, she felt her chin lift and her lips part before the totally male taste of him shattered her senses.

Like a merry-go-round moving ever so slowly, Christina stood stock-still, her breath stuck somewhere in the middle of her chest as his lips made a soft, thorough foray of hers.

Heat rushed through her body, setting off tingling explosions along her skin, behind her eyes, even in the tips of her fingers. Mindlessly, she began to kiss him back, began to want and need the connection to continue.

She was drifting to some sweet, heavenly place when he finally lifted his head. The shock of the separation instantly jerked her back to the reality of the dimly lit hallway and his serious face lingering just above hers.

Licking her burning lips, she hauled in a hoarse breath. "Maybe you ought to explain what that was all about."

With a forefinger beneath her chin, he closed her mouth, then traced the curve of her upper lip. "You might not be looking for a man, Christina, but I'm looking for a woman. And I'm trying to figure out if the woman I'm looking for is you."

Chapter Four

Confusion swirled inside Christina. She couldn't deny it was flattering to have a sexy man like Lex attracted to her. Yet she realized the foolishness of taking him seriously. He could have most any woman he crooked his finger at. Besides, her work was her life now, she reminded herself. Mike had cured her of trusting another man with her happiness.

"I'm sorry, but I'm not for the taking," she said quietly.

The disappointment that flashed in his eyes was at complete odds with the teasing curve to his lips. "Who says?"

She'd already heard through the ranch's rumor mill that he was every bit as much a playboy as his flirtatious manner implied. And she supposed some women would find him an exciting challenge. But Christina had learned the hard way that changing a man's fundamental values was impossible.

"I do. I didn't come here for your entertainment."

Shaking his head with dismay, he said, “I wasn’t thinking of you as my entertainment, Christina.”

His kiss had been like a violent earthquake to her. But not for anything would she let him know the upheaval going on inside her. It was too embarrassing.

“Really? I got the impression you think I hand kisses out like chocolate drops,” she said dully. Then, turning away from him, she pushed through the kitchen doors.

He was quick to follow, and she tried her best to ignore his giant presence as she walked over to their waiting supper, which was laid out on the long pine table.

“Christina, I suppose I should apologize to you. But I wanted that kiss. I snatched it. And it felt too damn good to feel sorry about. I do apologize if I upset you.”

She was making too much of an issue out of the kiss, she told herself. The best way to deal with it and him was to keep things light. But how could she do that when the taste of his lips had woken some sort of latent hunger inside her? Now, each time she glanced at his face, all she could think about was kissing him. “At least you’re honest—I appreciate that.”

He eased down in the space across from her. Then, after studying her for long, tense moments, he released a heavy breath. “Do you think I’m a bad guy or something?”

Christina reached for her napkin and hated the fact that her fingers were still trembling. She didn’t want to be vulnerable to any man. Especially a devil-may-care guy like Lex Saddler.

Keeping her eyes averted from his, she smoothed the piece of white linen across her lap. “No. I’ve heard rumors about you, but I don’t deal in rumors. I make up my own mind about people.”

“Rumors? Who’s been talking about me?”

"No one in particular," she said carefully. "But I've made my way around the stables, and some of the hands have tossed a few innuendos around. You have a reputation for liking the ladies."

His brows arched innocently. "Is anything wrong with that?"

There wasn't anything wrong with his fondness for women. He could have all the girlfriends he wanted. That was his business. Just as long as he didn't decide to lump her into the same herd.

"Not as far as I'm concerned. That's your business." She forced out a pent-up breath as he passed her a small wooden bowl filled with Caesar salad. "And as far as you and me and that kiss—let's just forget it and eat our supper. Okay?"

A sheepish smile slowly crept across his face. "I'm happy to hear you're not going to hold it against me for being a red-blooded man."

She rolled her eyes while trying to forget the feel of his lips moving against hers. "As long as you remember that the connection between us is only business, we'll get along just fine."

When he had kissed her a few minutes ago, her giving lips certainly hadn't felt like business only, Lex thought. But he wasn't about to point out that little issue to her now. He didn't want a mad hornet on his hands.

Digging into his own salad, he wondered what was coming over him. It wasn't his style to steal a kiss. He didn't usually *have* to steal them. Normally, his female counterparts were more than willing to share in a bit of physical pleasure.

But it was becoming plain to him that Christina Logan was totally different from the women he'd known in the past. She wasn't amused or charmed by his mere attention. No. He was going to have to show her that there was more to him than a wink and a grin and a few nights of bliss between the sheets.

"You might think that way, Christina, but I can't. I already consider you my friend."

Her attention remained on her salad, but he could see the stiff line of her shoulders visibly relax. She looked extra feminine tonight in a white peasant blouse and a tiered skirt of yellow printed calico. Her red hair was looped atop her head and clamped at the back with a tortoiseshell barrette. Silver hoops dangled from her ears, and the tiny cross she always wore dangled near the hint of cleavage exposed by the low neckline of her blouse. Just looking at her set his senses on fire.

"I can handle being your friend, Lex."

But nothing more. She might as well have spoken the words out loud, because he could feel them hanging in the air between them. And for some reason, Lex didn't understand; he felt totally deflated.

"I, um, I'm sorry if you thought...well, that I was thinking you were a man hunter like your mother," he said awkwardly. "I mean, not that being like your mother is a bad thing, but—"

She looked up at him. "You don't need to tiptoe around the truth, Lex. There's no way of saying it kindly. Being like my mother is not a compliment."

"Is that why you've never married?" he asked more soberly than he'd intended. "Because your mother has been through so many marriages?"

"Obviously, marriage isn't a sacred union to her," she said, with a hint of sarcasm, then shook her head. "I shouldn't have said that. Mother did try—she and Father remained together for fifteen years."

He swallowed a bite of salad before he pointed out, "You didn't exactly answer my question about why you haven't married."

"How do you know I haven't been married before?" she asked.

Lex shrugged. "I don't. I just assumed. Have you?"

She glanced away from him, but not before he spotted sad shadows in her eyes, shadows that could only have been put there by a man. And for a split second, Lex wished he'd not asked her anything so personal. For some reason, he didn't want to think that she might have loved another man so much that she'd wanted to marry him.

"No," she answered. "I got close once. But it didn't work out, and now that I look back on that relationship, I realize I made an escape." Sighing, she turned her blue eyes back to him. "To answer your question, I suppose a therapist would say my mother has warped my view of marriage. But in my opinion, that's hardly the reason that I'm still a single woman. I just haven't met the right man. A man that wants the same things I want."

From what she'd said before, he knew she believed love was the essential ingredient for marriage. She was obviously a romantic, who still believed there was some man out there who'd perfectly meet all her requirements. Well, he was a romantic, too. He'd always wanted to find love. But while he understood how to do all the gentle, flowery things that impressed most women, as for love? Other than his family, he'd never met anyone who even made him consider placing that much importance on another human being. He'd tried, but it had just never happened.

"Maybe your mother isn't looking for love, Christina," he suggested. "Could be that she's searching for financial security. Some women value that above everything."

She pushed aside her salad bowl and reached for the main course, a piping hot casserole dish full of lasagna.

"Money is something that Mother has never lacked. She has plenty to last her the rest of her life. No, her lifestyle stems from—other issues," she added glumly.

Christina's disclosure more than surprised Lex, although, he wasn't exactly sure why. Rich folks in South Texas were as common as mosquitoes after a summer rain. Still, he'd not expected to discover that Christina had come from a wealthy family. She didn't seem the pampered sort. Especially knowing that she'd worked in law enforcement for nine years. But then, he had to remember that his own sisters hardly needed to work to support themselves, yet Nicci filled her days with doctoring patients, and Mercedes had served eight years in the military. Money or not, everyone needed a purpose.

"Well, as far as Mom goes, she's not looking to Wolfe Maddson for security, either. I guess she thinks she loves the man," he added skeptically.

"Thinks? Lex, Geraldine is not the sort of woman who would marry for any other reason. Surely you can't think otherwise."

He ladled lasagna onto his plate. "No. But I—" He looked at her and wondered why he was talking to her about such things at all. Family issues were something he never discussed with girlfriends. But something about Christina seemed to pull things from his mouth before he even realized he was going to say them.

"Well, I'll just come out and say it," he went on. "It irks me to think that she could possibly care for the senator in the way that she did my father. Can you understand that?"

Her features softened. "Very much. But you shouldn't be thinking in those terms, Lex. From what I can see, no man could take your father's place in Geraldine's heart. She's only making room for a new love."

"I do want her to be happy," he admitted. "And for a long time now, I could tell she was lonely."

She had to admit that Lex Saddler was a walking contradiction. His actions implied that he didn't want to be a family man, yet he was just that. He'd devoted his life to a family job. She could see from his words and actions that his sisters and his mother, even his cousins, were more important to him than anything. So why wasn't he married? Was he turned off by the idea of a wife?

Forget those questions, Christina. Toss them out the window with the rest of your foolish dreams.

"I guess having your kids around doesn't fill all the gaps," he added wryly.

"No," she sadly agreed. "If it did, Retha wouldn't be working on husband number seven."

Nearly a week later, just before sundown, Lex and Matt were riding home from a far west pasture, where they'd been searching most of the afternoon for a bull that had failed to appear with his usual herd. It was past supper time, and Lex figured Christina and his mother had already eaten without him.

That was more than okay with him, Lex thought a bit crossly. Sitting across from Christina, mooning after her like some sick little bull calf who'd lost his mother, was not his style. He needed to snap out of this mental fog he'd been in since the P.I. had arrived. So what if she wasn't interested in falling into his arms? She would soon be gone from the ranch, anyway, and then she'd just become a dim memory.

As the horses picked their way through prickly pear and green briars, Matt said, "I don't know about you, but I'm dog tired. When we get back to the ranch, I'm going to try to talk Juliet into giving me a back rub."

"Humph," Lex snorted. "I doubt you'd end up getting any rest after a back rub from your gorgeous wife."

A tired grin spread across Matt's face, and Lex felt a spurt of envy. What would it feel like to know that he was going home to a loving wife? That she'd be at the door waiting, with a kiss and a smile?

Hell, what was he pining about, anyway? Cook was always there to pinch him on the cheek and serve him a good meal. And she didn't give him any wifely orders with it, either.

"You could be right about that," Matt agreed, with a chuckle, then glanced thoughtfully over at him. "You've been awfully quiet on the ride back. I thought you were happy about finding the bull. You ought to be. We hadn't seen him in over a week, and you gave twenty-five thousand for him. I thought he was too damned skinny for a price like that, but I'll grant you, he's spreading out really nicely now."

Lex sighed. No one had ever accused him of looking unhappy before. Is that what Christina had done to him? If so, that was added proof that it didn't pay to concentrate on just one woman.

"Yeah," Lex replied. "I realize I took a chance on him, but I think he'll pay off in the long run."

They rode in silence for a few moments while behind them, the last fiery rays of sun slid below the flat horizon, leaving the whole countryside bathed in golden twilight. The day had been hot, and both men were covered in dust. Lex didn't know what he wanted most, food or a long, cold shower.

"So how is the investigation going into Uncle Paul's death?" Matt asked.

Up until now, Matt had hardly mentioned Christina or the reason she'd come to the Sandbur. His cousin had always been astute about not butting into private matters unless he was invited. Lex was glad he'd brought it up. He had been wondering what the other man was thinking about the whole situation.

"Christina has begun going through Dad's papers and things, but she's not said much about what she's found so far," Lex told him. "Hell, after nearly twelve years, how can anyone figure out how something happened?"

"Clue by clue, I suppose. How long do you expect this private investigator to hang around the ranch?"

Lex shrugged. That was something he'd been wondering, too. He'd just been getting used to Christina being in the house and around the ranch yard when she'd announced she had to return to San Antonio for a few days to do some follow-up work on another case. Supposedly, she would be back this evening, and he was amazed at just how much he wanted to see her again. While she'd been gone, the place hadn't been the same. He hadn't been the same. And that was an unsettling thought. Lex didn't want his happiness to depend solely on a woman.

"I have no idea. Christina hasn't mentioned any sort of timetable to me. And Mom is gone so much, I haven't had a chance to ask her. Maybe that's a good thing. I don't like talking to her about any of this."

Matt quietly studied him. "Why is that?"

Lex bit back a curse. "Because I think Mom should leave things alone. Let Dad rest in peace."

"But what if things didn't happen as the police think?" Matt asked. "Wouldn't you like to know?"

Dead or alive, I want, need to know! Christina's emotional statement about her missing brother drifted through Lex's mind like a whispered plea.

"I suppose. But digging up the past is painful to me. Dad

is gone. Whether he was killed or died from a heart attack, the truth won't bring him back."

"No. But it might bring justice to his memory."

Lex stared, with surprise, at his cousin. "Justice? You say that like you think he might have been murdered! Is that what you really believe?"

"I remember back before it happened, Lex. Uncle Paul seemed very distracted, and he'd lost so much weight that I was beginning to worry about him having some sort of disease."

All had not been right with your father.

His mother's remarks only reinforced what Matt was saying, and Lex felt shaken right down to the heels of his boots. He didn't want to think that anyone could have intentionally harmed his father. Paul had been such a gentle, caring human being. He'd loved everyone. Why would anyone have wanted to hurt him?

"He must have had a disease," Lex mumbled. "Coronary disease."

"But he'd just gone through a complete physical with his family doctor," Matt pointed out. "They would have discovered if anything was physically wrong with him."

Lex tugged on the brim of his dusty straw hat. "You're only thinking in sinister terms because of what happened to Uncle Mingo. You think because someone nearly killed your own father that it must have happened to mine, too."

"I'm not thinking anything of the sort!" Matt retorted. "The thugs who attacked Dad didn't have murder on their mind, obviously. Otherwise, they wouldn't have left him breathing."

Releasing another long breath, Lex lifted his gaze toward the pink and gold sky. "There must be something about the Sandbur, Matt, that draws misfortune," he said pensively.

"Our grandfather was murdered. Your first wife was killed in a horse accident. Your father was mugged, beaten and left for dead. Then my father died in a suspicious accident. Little Marti was kidnapped. What next?"

"Lex, it's not the Sandbur that causes these things," Matt said sagely. "It's life. Pure and simple."

Lex grimaced. "Then you ought to tell Mom that," he said sourly. "Then maybe she'd send Christina Logan back to San Antonio—for good."

Matt's black brows pulled together with confusion. "What's the matter? Don't you like the woman?"

Hell, why had he said such a thing? Lex wondered. He didn't want Christina to go anywhere. The past few days without her had been awful. He'd gotten attached to her company and for the first time in his life, he missed being with a woman. And that reluctance of hers was getting to him more than anything. He didn't want to have to seduce her. He wanted it to be her own idea to want him. But there was no need to let his cousin know how soppy he was beginning to feel for the private investigator. After all, nothing would likely come of it. Especially when she seemed dead set against having any sort of relationship with him.

"I like her well enough," Lex said shortly. "Now do you think we can kick up these horses? I'm damn nigh starving."

It was after eight o'clock that evening before Lex finally showered and then headed down to the kitchen to find himself something to eat. Cook was already gone for the evening, but she'd left him a covered plate on the stove, with a note containing instructions on how long to leave it in the microwave.

He'd bring her a rose in the morning, at breakfast, Lex

decided as he waited for the fried chicken and accompanying vegetables to heat. Hattie would like that. And he liked letting the woman know how much he loved her.

And what about Christina? he asked himself. Why didn't he try offering her a rose? Because she wouldn't want it, he thought dourly. She wanted things between them to be proper and platonic. Damn it. He had to change her mind. Somehow. Someway.

Once the plate of food was heated, he decided he didn't want to eat alone in the kitchen. Memories of the last meal he'd shared with Christina were still too fresh in his mind, so he stepped out a back door, with intentions of eating on the patio.

To his surprise, he found Christina and his mother sitting in the semidarkness, exchanging words in a low tone, which became even lower when they spotted his approach.

Lex watched his mother exchange an odd look with Christina, then straighten upright in her chair.

"I see you finally made it back to the house," Geraldine said to him. "Did you find the bull?"

Lex greeted both women, then carried his plate over to a nearby table. As he pulled up a redwood chair, he answered his mother's question. "We found the bull. He was down in the river bottoms, minding his own business. Didn't appear to be a thing wrong with him. I guess he just needed to be away from the womenfolks for a while."

"Maybe they needed to be away from him," Christina suggested dryly.

He rested his eyes on her and felt his heart thump with pleasure at seeing her again. "Believe me, they'll want his company sooner or later."

He picked up a chicken leg and chomped into it, while a

few feet away from him, Geraldine cleared her throat, then abruptly rose to her feet.

"If you two will excuse me," she said, "I have things in the house to do."

Lex stared after his mother as she quickly walked away, then turned his attention back to Christina. "It's nice to have you back on the ranch. Did you make any headway on the other case you're working?"

She nodded. "Thanks for asking. I found the man I was looking for, and thankfully, he'll be able to testify for a person my friend is defending."

His brows peaked with interest. "You have a friend that's a criminal lawyer?"

"Yes. Olivia Mills. You'd like her."

Lex grinned. "Is she pretty?"

"She's beautiful and intelligent."

"Like you, then."

She glanced away from him, and Lex could see that his simple comment troubled her. But why? He thought women were supposed to like compliments, but he was learning more and more that Christina wasn't the norm.

When she failed to make any sort of reply, Lex turned his attention to eating, but after a few bites, he couldn't remain silent. "What's the matter with Mom? She practically ran back into the house."

"She has a lot on her mind."

Grimacing, he reached for the beer he'd carried out with him. "You two were discussing something when I walked up. What was it? Me?"

She groaned. "You must think *everything* revolves around you."

Odd that she should say that. If anything, Lex had always

thought exactly the opposite. He was the middle child and the only male, at that. Lex had always felt that his mother focused more on his two sisters. In spite of all her good qualities, Geraldine could be a hard woman. Sometimes she could make Lex feel as if he was little more than a glorified ranch hand, rather than her son.

"Not hardly. I got the impression that she was talking about something she wasn't keen on me hearing. What was it? Dad's case?"

She let out a heavy breath. "Yes. But she was too upset to go into it with you tonight."

He took several bites of food as he waited for her to elaborate. When she didn't, he finally prompted, "So? What about Dad's case? You've uncovered something that upset her?"

Rising from the rattan chair, he watched her move aimlessly across the brick patio. Tonight she was a slim picture in white slacks and a black-and-white tropical-print blouse. Her bright copper hair was fixed in a curly mass on the crown of her head. She not only looked beautiful, he realized, but she also moved with a lithe grace, which only intensified the sexual aura surrounding her. He took a minute to just admire her, enjoying the chance to watch her again after the too-long days she'd spent away from him.

She said, "I told Geraldine that the more I study the police reports and couple them with what you've told me about Paul's friends, the more suspicious I get about his death."

Mixed feelings swirled through Lex as he considered Christina's suggestion. Since he'd talked with Matt on the ride home, he'd been telling himself he needed to keep an open mind about this whole matter. Yet to think the three men that he remembered as friends of the family might have done his father harm was almost too far-fetched to imagine. He hated the uneasy feeling in his stomach, and it made him lash out.

"So why was she upset about this news? For the sake of Dad's memory? Or because it might ruin her marriage plans to Wolfe?"

Christina stopped in her tracks long enough to glare at him. "What a horrible, cruel thing to say!"

Disgusted with himself and with her, he reached up and swiped a heavy hand through his hair. "Maybe it was," he admitted, "but I'm only trying to be honest with you and myself. If she's going to dig up this painful time in our lives, I wish she'd do it for herself and her family. Not for Wolfe Maddson."

Even in the dim lighting he could see disappointment on her face. It was not the sort of expression he wanted to garner from this woman.

"It's obvious you don't understand anything about being in love."

"And you do?"

She stared at him for a few long, awkward moments and then turned her back to him. "Look, Lex, right now you need to put Wolfe Maddson out of the equation. Yes, Geraldine loves him, but she also loved your father. It's very upsetting to her to think that people Paul trusted might have harmed him."

Ignoring the last bites of food on his plate, Lex rose to his feet and went to stand behind her. "We'll talk about Dad's case in a minute. Right now, I'd like you to answer my question," he said quietly.

As he waited for her to reply, he could hear a nearby choir of frogs warming up for their nightly performance. Down by the bunkhouse, faint sounds of laughter mingled with accordion-laden Tejano music. A warm, heavy breeze rustled the honeysuckle vines above their heads and swirled the sweet aroma around them like a soft cloud.

It was a hot, humid night. Just perfect for making love. His thoughts drifted to the woman standing next to him and he felt his libido begin to stir.

"My love life doesn't pertain to any of this," she finally said.

"It does when you start lecturing me on the subject."

She glanced over her shoulder at him. "It's obvious that you resent the idea of your mother loving a man other than your father."

In spite of her jarring words, Lex found his senses distracted by her nearness. Even as he told himself not to touch her, his hands itched to settle on her shoulders. "I didn't realize you were a psychologist along with a private investigator. When did you acquire that degree?"

Slowly, she turned to face him. "Cutting me down won't change the facts, Lex."

"All right, I'm a selfish bastard. Is that what you want to hear me say? That I have no compassion or understanding for my mother's feelings?"

"Do you?"

He muttered a curse in frustration. How could he explain that it felt better to let himself believe his father had died accidentally? How could he make her see that he couldn't bear to image his father dying violently, at the hands of someone else? "Of course I do. I want her to be happy. But I also have to wonder if she's stopped to think what this digging into the past is doing to the rest of the family. Does she care?"

"Perhaps you should ask her that."

He shook his head. "When my mother gets her head set on something, there's no changing it. No matter the consequences. And you being here isn't helping matters. Especially when you throw out little tidbits to make her believe you're onto something."

"I didn't throw her any tidbits! I only expressed my thoughts to her, which she asked for! What am I supposed to do? Lie and try to dissuade her from searching for the truth? Tell her that it's an impossible task and to forget it?" She shook her head. "I can't do that. And I don't know why you would want me to. Unless you're scared."

Lex stiffened. Of all the things he'd been accused of, especially by a woman, being cowardly wasn't one of them. Was she right? Was he scared? Scared of learning his father had been murdered. And scared of being around her every day and feeling himself falling deeper and deeper under her spell.

But he wasn't about to admit any such thing to her. He didn't even want to admit it to himself. "You're wrong," he insisted. "If you think I'm worried that you're going to dig up something criminal about my dad, you couldn't be more off base. He was a good man through and through. Deep down, I'm more certain of that than I am of my own name."

She tilted her chin a fraction upward. "If that's the case, then you must be making all of this fuss because you want me gone from here. Why?"

Desire wrapped around his frustration and finally pushed him to reach for her. As he folded his arms across her back and lowered his lips to hers, he whispered, "Maybe because I'm tired of not being able to do this."

Chapter Five

For the past week, Christina had been telling herself over and over that she was never going to kiss the man again. That she wasn't even going to give Lex Saddler the *chance* to kiss her a second time.

Yet the moment his arms had come around her and his lips had fastened over hers, she'd been as lost as a raindrop in a downpour.

Without stopping to think at all, she angled her head to match his and latched her fingers over the tops of his shoulders. Her response was countered with his hands on her back, drawing her tight against the front of his body.

The intimate contact swamped her body with heat, and she was certain her blood had turned to liquid fire as it swam through her veins at lightning speed. The taste of him was dark, wild and exciting, and too good to resist. With a tiny moan deep in her throat, she opened her mouth and accepted the insistent prod of his tongue against her teeth.

Sweat began to dampen her skin, then roll in tiny rivers between her breasts and into the waistband of her slacks, while the air in her lungs was slowly but surely disappearing. At the same time she could feel his hands kneading her back, then slipping lower and lower, until his palms were cupping the curve of her rear.

It wasn't until he hauled her hips tightly against his that reality hit her. Their kiss had gone beyond a meeting of lips. It was a sexual embrace that was rapidly leading her to a total meltdown.

Mustering all the strength she could find, she finally managed to drag her lips away from his and twist out of the heady circle of his arms.

Long moments passed before Christina was composed enough to speak, yet even then her voice was raw and husky.

"You like going against my wishes, don't you?"

He chuckled softly, and she felt his fingers tangling in the loose tendrils of hair sticking to the sweat on the back of her neck.

"Who are you trying to kid?" he asked in a low voice. "You wanted that kiss as much as I did."

The fact that he was so right only made her feel more frustrated with herself. Yet even as she told herself she should step away from him, the touch of his fingers was luring her, seducing her. "Okay. Earlier you were trying to be honest with me," she said huskily. "So I'll admit that I—" She forced herself to turn back to him. The dark shadows slanting across his face gave his rough-hewed features an even more rakish look, and she was forced to swallow hard before she managed to finish speaking. "I find you very attractive. And there must be some sort of—chemistry between us."

"Must be? Oh, baby, we're like two matches striking off each other."

Yes, she felt like a match that had just exploded into flames. Heat was still tingling in her hands and cheeks, her breasts and loins. It was scandalous how her body had reacted to his.

"Setting a fire isn't always a good thing," she tried to reason. "It could get out of control."

"Yeah. But I'd rather be singed by a wildfire than frozen by a blizzard."

Turning away from him, she walked over to the edge of the patio and wiped a hand across her damp brow. Never in her life, not even with Mike, had she ever had one kiss fill her with such longing. When she'd had her hands on Lex's shoulders, when his hard, warm body had been pressed against hers, it had felt right and good. As though he'd been made for her and she for him.

But that thinking was crazy, she mentally warned herself, and she had to stop it before her heart got all mixed up with physical desire. She was here on the Sandbur to do a job and nothing else.

Once again she felt him walking up behind her, and this time when his hand touched her shoulder, a thick lump filled her throat.

"I wish you wouldn't run away from me, Christina."

She was probably a fool, but there was something in his voice that sounded almost vulnerable, that drew her to him in a way that frightened her. But she was determined to resist it—and him.

"I'm not running from you." Bracing herself with a deep

breath, she turned to meet his gaze. "In fact, I was about to ask you if you might take off work one day this week and take a little trip with me."

Her suggestion floored him so much that for a moment or two he didn't speak.

"A trip with you? Are you kidding me?"

Suddenly feeling as though a tight band had been lifted from her heart, she laughed softly. "No. I'm serious. I'd like for the two of us to drive down to Corpus Christi."

He placed his palm against her forehead. "I think I should call Nicci and have her come over here and examine you. A bug or something must have bitten you."

She'd been bitten all right, but it wasn't by any bug. "I feel very well at the moment. And I need you."

Impish grooves appeared near the corners of his mouth. "Now you're talking, honey. That's exactly what I wanted to hear."

How could a woman resist a man who was so playful and sweet? It was impossible, she thought. It was even more impossible to keep a smile from curving her lips.

"I was talking about your mind," she told him. "And your mental support."

He must have sensed the change that had come over her in the past few moments, because he seemed to know that she wouldn't pull away when his hands rested gently on top of her shoulders.

"I've never had a woman want me for my mind," he said, with a chuckle, then his expression sobered as he brushed the back of his forefinger beneath her chin. "I think I kinda like the idea. And who knows, you might just get to needing the rest of me."

Everything inside her was turning to a melting, quivering mass, and she had to fight to prevent her arms from sliding around his neck, her mouth from seeking his.

Clearing her throat, she said, "And you might decide I'm not worth the effort." Before he could make a reply to that, she eased a step back from him and quickly added, "The trip is about Paul. Not you and me."

Lex was hardly about to let that squash his optimism. No matter what she said, he'd felt things in her kiss that she couldn't deny. Longing and hunger and a plea for him to appease those needs. But was making love to this woman all he really wanted? No, he wouldn't think about that now. He didn't want to think anymore tonight; he simply wanted to enjoy having her home again.

"I'd already concluded that."

"Then you agree to go?"

As if he could deny her anything, Lex thought wryly. One long, hot embrace with the woman had left him feeling like her puppet. It was downright scary, but in a very irresistible way.

"I do. But I am curious as to what you think this trip will accomplish. Besides a pleasant visit to the beach."

She gave him a short smile. "I've discovered that the same bait house where your father and his friends regularly bought bait is still in existence. I'd like to question anyone that might have remembered seeing the quartet that day or even on any of their other fishing trips."

"The police didn't do this originally?"

"There's one brief interview on record with a man working at the bait house, but it was hardly enough to satisfy my curiosity."

"You can't do this over the telephone?"

This time her smile was patient. "I'd rather do my questioning face-to-face. You can pick up on things that you'd miss over the telephone."

"I see. But don't you think it's doubtful that anyone would still be working at that same bait house after nearly twelve years?"

She shrugged. "You have to start somewhere. If not, we'll hopefully find someone from the shop still living in the city. Besides, that's not all I want to do. I also want to charter a boat to take us out to the coordinates where Red, Harve and Lawrence said your father went overboard. At least, the coordinates they gave to the police."

Lex's mind was suddenly jerked away from the lingering pleasure of her kiss. "Why in the world is that important? There's nothing out there but water!"

"You've been there?" she questioned.

"Well, no. Seeing where my father died isn't particularly something I've ever wanted to do."

She reached out and curled her hand over his forearm. The feel of her fingers against his skin was oddly comforting and provocative at the same time.

"You don't have to go on the boat with me. But I need to get a sense of where Paul and his friends were fishing at the time of the incident. How far they were away from land or a shipping lane where boats might have been passing."

Lex grimaced. "The police report stated that no one else witnessed the accident."

"According to Paul's friends," she replied. "They also state that they radioed the Coast Guard for help, but if you look at the time that call was made and the time they arrived on shore, they're only a few minutes apart. That doesn't jive with me."

"I don't find that overly suspicious. Could be the men

were too caught up in trying to pull Dad from the water t
think about calling anyone."

"Could be. But I want to take a look down there just th
same. When do you think you might be free to go?"

"Tomorrow, I have a buyer coming to look at bulls. An
Thursday, we're starting a roundup for a herd of cattle I'v
sold to a ranch in Florida. Then on Saturday, Matt wants m
to go with him to an auction."

"So that means you won't be free until Sunday?" sh
asked.

"I'm sorry, Christina. This is a particularly busy week fo
me."

Her expression turned thoughtful. "Don't worry about it
I've got a busy schedule, too. Something has come up o
another case that requires me to go back to San Antonio
While I'm there, I'm going to use any extra time I have t
try to interview Red, Harve and Lawrence."

She had to leave again. The news disappointed him. An
the idea of her going alone to see his dad's old boatin
buddies left him a little uneasy.

His fingers curled around her upper arm, then slid slowl
to her elbow. "Are you sure you have to go back so soon?
he asked. "You just got back here."

Her gaze flickered shyly away from his, and Le
wondered if she was thinking about their kiss. The ide
stirred him almost as much as touching her. Yet he realize
that now wasn't the time to press her for another. Hopefull
if he gave her time to think about the two of them togethe
she'd begin to come to terms with wanting him as much a
he wanted her.

Her gaze traveled back to his, and this time he could se

a soft light flickering in the blue orbs, tenderness bending the corners of her lips. He didn't know what he'd done to find a bit of favor in her sight, but whatever it had been, he hoped to hell he could repeat it.

"I'm afraid so," she answered. "Work calls. But if all goes well, I'll be back here Thursday evening."

To Lex, that sounded like an eternity. Especially when all he wanted to do was pull her into his arms and make slow, sweet love to her. "The roundup is going to be an overnighter, so I'll probably be out on the range when you return. But I'll catch up with you before our trip to Corpus."

She nodded, then cast him an awkward smile. "I'm glad you're going with me, Lex. And I'm glad you're not making a fuss about this."

He chuckled softly. "Why would any man make a fuss about taking a trip with a beautiful woman?" he asked teasingly, and then suddenly his smile faded and his voice turned sober. "These past few days I've decided I want to prove to anyone and everyone that no matter how Dad died, he was always a good, honest man."

Her fingers reached up and squeezed his forearm. "Whatever your motives, it's good that you want to know the truth."

That bit of praise caused his gaze to drop awkwardly to the toes of his boots, which only made Lex feel more like an idiot. Compliments from other women rolled off his back like rain on an oiled duster. At thirty-five, he'd been to town more than once, and he was wise enough to know that it was easy for the opposite sex to say pretty words when it suited their cause. So why did he believe Christina's were sincere? Why did they leave him feeling sheepish and susceptible?

Because she was that sort of woman. The honest, open

kind. The kind that made good daughters, wives, mothers and sisters. The family kind.

Lifting his gaze back to hers, he said, "I've been thinking about your brother, Christina. Do you believe you'll ever find him? Or do you think that he's…not alive anymore?"

A pensive shadow fell over her lovely features. "In my darkest moments, I fear that he's gone. But then I hear of other cases where missing people have been found alive after many years and my hope bubbles up all over again."

His heart suddenly ached for her. "Hope is a good thing, Christina."

"Yes, and I'm doing my best to hang on to mine." She carefully eased her arm away from his grasp. "I need to go in now, so I'll say good night, Lex."

"Good night."

She turned and walked back to the house. As Lex watched her go, he realized he wanted her to be happy. He cared about her feelings, her life. So what did that make him? A sap? Or was he finally beginning to see what an emotional relationship with a woman could be?

Either way, the answers shook him. And what bothered him the most…was that he kind of liked it.

Two days later, just as the sun was dipping and the broiling temperature beginning to ease, Christina parked her car at the west end of the ranch house. She was tired. The past two days had been filled with frustration and roadblocks of every imaginable sort. The tip she'd had on the missing person's case had turned out to be fruitless, just wishful thinking by a desperate relative.

As for Paul Saddler's so-called friends, she'd not been able to catch up with any of the three. Red Winters had been away on a trip to Vegas with his second wife. Harve Dirksen had been out of town on a business trip. The maid who'd answered his door had told Christina that her boss was a land developer and had his hand in building strip malls.

As for Lawrence Carter, she'd only been able to talk to his wife. Second wife, that is. A large, blustery woman with a poodle dog under each arm. From what Christina could gather from her, Lawrence now worked as an investment advisor for a local bank in San Antonio. Only he'd been sent to Dallas, to a sister bank, and wouldn't be home for another week.

Usually, Christina expected her job to include such delays and obstacles. She made it a point to never let them get under her skin. But these past two days, her work had only been a part of the reason for the weariness settling over her. The whole time she'd been in San Antonio, her mind had been on Lex. She'd missed him and imagined him in every possible scenario, including being in her arms, kissing her the way he'd kissed her beneath the arbor of honeysuckle.

Trying to shake away that tempting thought, she fetched a small leather duffel from the trunk of the car and entered the house by way of the kitchen.

She found the usually busy room empty, with everything cleaned and in perfect order. A note from Cook was attached to the refrigerator, telling her that Geraldine was out of town, Lex was on roundup and that there was a shepherd's pie in the fridge if she wanted to heat it.

Sighing, Christina left the kitchen and headed upstairs to her room. The house felt so empty without Lex. And even though she'd known that he'd be away on roundup this evening, a tiny part of her had hoped he would remember she'd be arriving and take the time to be here to greet her. But that was foolish thinking. The ranch was huge, and he was probably miles and miles from the house. He had lots of work to do, and she wasn't that important to him.

Do you want to be that important to him?

As Christina stepped out of her linen dress and tossed it on the bed, she was trying to answer that question, trying to convince herself she wasn't falling for Lex Saddler when a knock suddenly sounded on her bedroom door.

"Christina? Are you in there?"

Lex's unexpected voice jolted her, and she hastily reached for a silk robe and headed to the door.

"Yes! Uh…just a moment." She fumbled with the tie at her waist, then made sure she was modestly covered before she partially opened the door and stuck her head out. "Lex, what are you doing here? I thought you'd be out with the other wranglers."

His gaze slipped to the spot between her breasts, where her hand was gripping the edges of the robe together, then back to her face. "I was out with the men. I'm sorry if I caught you at a bad moment. Have you been here long?"

"All of ten minutes, maybe. Why?"

He suddenly smiled, and Christina felt the weight of the past couple of days melting away.

"Then you haven't eaten?"

"No. But I'm not that hungry."

He laughed, and she realized it was a sound that she'd missed, a sound that filled her with good feelings.

"You will be. Pull on a pair of jeans and boots, and meet me out on the patio in five minutes. I'm going to take you to a bona fide cowboy cookout." As he turned away from the door, he tossed over his shoulder, "And bring a bag with whatever you can't do without for one night."

"A bag? What for?" Christina called after him.

As he headed down the hallway to the staircase, he called back to her. "Tonight we're going to sleep out under the stars."

Sleep under the stars? Was he crazy? Or was she crazier for following his orders? she wondered as she hurried to the closet to find a pair of jeans.

Minutes later, the two of them were in one of the ranch's work trucks, barreling across rough pastureland. As they jostled their way toward the spot near the river where the men had camped, it dawned on Christina that Lex hadn't once asked her about what, if any, information she'd found in San Antonio. And to her surprise, she realized that she was glad he wanted to be with her for no other reason than her company.

"It would have been nicer to have ridden out here on horseback," he said as he steered the truck around a patch of blooming prickly pear. "But since we didn't have time for that, we'll have to do it another time."

Another time. Did he think there would be other times they'd be together? she wondered. Did he think that once her job was finished, she'd ever return to the Sandbur? No. She didn't want to think about that now. Tonight she was on an adventure, and she was going to enjoy it.

"Do you have roundups often?" she asked, her gaze sliding over to where he sat behind the steering wheel. His jeans and gray chambray shirt were dusty, and his hat was so coated, it looked more brown than black. Spurs were strapped to his boots, and between them on the seat lay a pair of worn bat-wing chaps. He was in his element, she realized, and doing something he was born and bred to do.

"Three or four times a year. Depending on how many cattle we decide to sell." He pointed to a spot in the distance. "There's the camp. And if the men have already eaten, they'd damned sure better have left us some cobbler."

As they grew nearer, Christina could see an actual chuck wagon with a canvas cover and a campfire with several men milling around it. Nearby, a dozen or more horses were tethered to a picket line. Christina recognized one of them as Leo, the paint that Lex usually rode. Saddles and horse blankets dotted the ground, and the smell of burning mesquite and strong coffee filled the air. It was a scene right out of the western movies Christina often watched.

Since she'd spent some time exploring around the ranch yard, she'd met most of the hands that were working the roundup. The ones she'd not met, Lex quickly introduced to her, then wasted no time in leading her over to the chuck wagon, where they filled red granite plates with the traditional cowboy fare of steak, potatoes and barbecued beans.

"Let's take our meal down by the river," he suggested. "It might be a bit cooler there."

"Lead the way," she told him.

The riverbank was steep, but once they reached the bottom, the ground leveled out to a sandy wash shaded by willows and salt cedars. Lex found a short piece of fallen log to use for a seat, forcing them to sit close together as they ate the hearty food.

"It's so nice and quiet out here," Christina said, with a sigh. "No traffic or technical gadgets ringing or beeping."

"That's what I like about it the most. When I have to travel and jump from one plane to the next or answer a dozen messages left on my phone, I long to get back on the ranch and in the solitude like this. 'Course, I suppose it would get boring for a woman like you."

Not if I'm with the right person. Keeping that thought to herself, she said, "I'm not easily bored, Lex. I love the outdoors."

He glanced at her. "Do you live on acreage in San Antonio?"

She smiled wanly. "No. I live in an apartment, not far from the office where I work."

"You like living in the city?"

"I've never thought about it. I've always lived there."

"Your parents were city folks?"

Nodding, she said, "Dad's parents owned a chain of successful nightclubs across Texas, and he was involved in that business for years. Mom came from an oil family. Besides the oil, her parents also owned a construction company, so both my parents never lacked for money. They could have purchased all sorts of country property, but that wasn't their style."

"So you weren't interested in following in those family businesses?"

Shaking her head, she said, "By the time I became old enough to think about a career, my grandparents were dying off. My parents didn't bother trying to pass their legacies on to their children. I suppose it was because neither was very interested in what they did or where their money came from. They weren't like your parents, Lex. You've had a family legacy passed on to you from generation to generation. You have a solid foundation beneath your feet, and you appreciate that. It's something for you to be proud of."

His smile was gentle as he reached up and squeezed her shoulder, and for a moment, Christina feared her eyes were going to fill with tears.

"Well, someday you'll have children of your own, and you can do things better for them."

Would she have children? After her breakup with Mike, she'd practically given up on having a family. She'd been trying to convince herself that a career as an investigator was enough to keep her life full. Yet since she'd met Lex, thoughts of children, a home and a husband kept creeping into her dreams. Now, each time she walked into her apartment, it felt totally empty. Darn it. Why was she letting this man toy with her heart and all the plans she'd tried to make for herself?

"Uh, Christina? You've gone quiet. Have I said something wrong? You don't want children?"

A bit embarrassed for letting him catch her daydreaming, she busied herself with slicing into a hunk of rare rib eye. "I'd love to have children. Someday. When I meet the right man." She dared to glance up at him. "What about you? Do you ever plan to have children? You have so much to pass on to them."

He looked out across the river, and for the first time since she'd met him, Christina spotted a crack of uncertainty in his armor. "I think about it sometimes. But I'm not sure I'd be good at being a parent."

"I expect no one is sure—before they take on the job. But I can't see why you'd question yourself. You've had great examples to follow."

He grimaced. "Yeah, that's just it. Dad was a great parent. I can't think of a time he ever disappointed me. I'm not sure I could ever live up to his standard." He released a heavy breath, then turned a faint smile on her. "Besides, you have to meet the right woman to want children."

"And that's never happened? You've never met a woman who's made you think of having a family?"

A coy smile suddenly curved one side of his lips. "What would you say if I said I might be looking at her now?"

Christina's heart was thumping so hard and fast, she was certain he could probably see the front of her shirt shaking. "I'd say a mosquito has probably bitten you and given you a fever," she purposely teased.

The smile on his lips remained, but there was a soberness in his eyes that shook her right to the core of her being.

"I'll take an aspirin and look at you again in the morning," he murmured.

She was wondering how she could respond to that when the sound of a guitar being strummed drifted over them.

Glad for the distraction, she glanced over her shoulder and said, "It sounds like we're going to have entertainment tonight."

"That's Eduardo. He's the only one of the bunch brave enough to play and sing." He rose from the log and reached down for her hand. "Come on. If you're ready, we'll go back and find a good seat for the concert."

Back at the campground, the two of them topped their meal off with apple cobbler and cups of strong coffee, then took seats on the ground and used a wagon wheel for a backrest.

As night fell and the stars became visible in the wide Texas sky, Christina forgot about everything but Lex and sharing this part of his life, even if it was only for one night.

After a while, Lex's lips bent near to her ear. "Do you know what Eduardo is singing now?" he asked.

The song was in Spanish, but since Christina knew the language fluently, she had no trouble following the lyrics. "He's singing about a woman who ran away and left all her riches behind just to be with her lover—the gypsy Davey."

It was an erotic tune, especially for a trail song, and hearing it only made Christina more aware of Lex's strong arm next to hers, his long legs stretched out in front of him. And before she could stop herself, her head listed sideways and nestled comfortably on his strong shoulder.

Next to her ear, she heard him sigh, and the sound tumbled right through her heart.

* * *

By the time Sunday morning rolled around, Christina was still thinking about her night spent on the roundup. Lex had taken great pains to make her a comfortable bed an arm's length away from his. She'd lain there in the dying firelight, gazing at his profile and thinking how exciting and full a life with him would be.

But morning had brought reality back with a jerk. After a hasty breakfast, Lex had saddled up Leo for a day's work, and she'd driven the truck back to the ranch to begin her diligent sifting through Paul Saddler's papers. Since that time, she'd only spoken with Lex briefly. At that time he'd assured her he'd be ready for the trip to Corpus.

This morning, as Christina waited for him to join her on the front porch, the temperature hovered near eighty degrees. Cool shorts and a halter top would have felt good, but she'd decided a simple cotton sheath splashed with flowers in pale yellow and lime green would be more appropriate.

Since they'd be spending most of the day on the coast, she'd wondered if Lex would forgo his boots and jeans and hat, but when he finally appeared, she saw that the only concession he'd made was a white polo shirt. Even so, he looked rakishly handsome as he took his place behind the wheel of his personal truck.

Christina wasn't sure if the accelerated beat of her heart was due to his close presence or the fact that the two of them were headed out on an unpredictable journey.

"You haven't forgotten anything, have you?" he asked as they passed under the huge entrance of the ranch yard.

She patted a small briefcase lying on the console between them. "Addresses and photos are all here. And I've already called ahead and scheduled the boat charter. They'll take us out at eleven. Or me out, if you prefer to stay ashore."

He glanced knowingly over at her. "I'm not about to let you go out alone on a boat with a group of strange men. Who knows what could happen."

His remark surprised her. She'd never expected him to want to protect her. Her parents certainly had never sheltered her. And even Mike, a veteran police officer, had never been particularly protective of her. He'd always believed she was capable of taking care of herself. And she liked to believe she was. Still, it was sweetly old-fashioned to have Lex wanting to be her defender.

"If I understood it right," she told him, "there'll only be one man accompanying me on the boat."

"Then I'm sure as hell going," he said sharply. "You can't trust anyone nowadays."

"I'm glad you're going," she admitted, then gave him a playful smile. "But who's going to be my bodyguard when I go back to work in San Antonio?"

Even though she'd been teasing, he didn't look as though he was when he said, "Maybe you should just stay, instead."

Chapter Six

An hour and a half later, the truck was climbing up the huge causeway spanning the ship channel on the north side of the city. To the left of them, the sun sparkled on Corpus Christi Bay and the docked World War II aircraft carrier, the USS *Lexington*, which now served as a museum. To their right, shipping barges chugged to and from loading docks, while directly in front of them, the skyline of the city carved niches from the green-blue ocean.

Lex exited onto Ocean Drive, and in a few short minutes, they were parked in front of a small, weathered building. The lapped siding looked like it had once been painted coral, but sand, wind and salt had since buffed it to a puny pink. Above the wooden screen door, a creaky sign read Ray's Bait.

As they walked across the small parking lot graveled with crushed oyster shells, Lex glanced doubtfully over at her. "I hate to be a pessimist, Christina, but this seems like a long shot."

"In my profession, long shots are things I often have to take. And when I sometimes win, the payoff is usually more than I ever expected."

He grunted. "I've never been much of a gambler."

"You put your fortune in livestock, which could fall over dead without warning or lose their value according to the whims of the market. I'd call that big-time gambling."

"You might think so," he said, with a vague smile. "It's just a way of life for me."

By now they'd reached the entrance to the building. Lex opened the screen door and allowed Christina to step through before he followed. Inside, the small interior was dim and smelled of fish, beer and burned coffee. To the immediate right, a long counter was equipped with a cash register and lined with jars of fishing lures and jigs. To the left, a separate room was outfitted with concrete tanks filled with bubbling water.

At the moment, a plump blond woman in her early twenties was dipping out tiny shad and placing the bait in a customer's foam bucket.

Christina and Lex waited to one side until she'd finished the task and taken the other man's money. Once he'd ambled out the door, Christina stepped up to the counter, while Lex hung back just behind her shoulder.

"Can I help y'all?" the young woman asked.

The young woman was chewing gum, and her long bangs were battling with her eyelashes for hanging space.

Clearing her throat, Christina said, "Uh, yes. We're looking for Ray Pena. Is he around?"

The young woman's brown eyes darted suspiciously from Christina to Lex and back again. "The owner? He's not here today. He had to go down to Falfurrias. Somethin' to do with his sister." She chewed on her bottom lip. "Is he in trouble?"

"Does trouble commonly follow Mr. Pena around?" Lex asked dryly.

The blonde shook her head. "No. But you two smell like cops to me. Sorta look like it, too."

Christina quickly interjected, "We're nothing of the sort. We're simply looking for some information. Will Mr. Pena be back tomorrow?"

"Said he would. Guess you could try again in the mornin'."

"We'll do that," Christina told her. "And thank you, Miss—"

"Sally. Sally Donner."

Christina smiled and reached to shake the woman's hand. "Thank you, Sally. It was nice meeting you."

"Yeah. Sure."

Christina and Lex walked outside, pausing several steps away from the open entrance to the bait house.

"What are we going to do now?" Lex asked. "I don't have time to drive down here tomorrow morning. Matt is expecting me to go with him to auction tomorrow afternoon."

She fished her sunglasses out of her purse and jammed them on her face. "If we stay here tonight and talk to Mr. Pena in the morning, you'll still have time to make the trip with your cousin."

Lex stared at her. "Stay here in Corpus tonight?"

"Do you have a better idea? Or would you rather drive down here again next week?"

He considered her questions for a moment, and then suddenly a grin spread across his face. "What the hell. I haven't stayed on the beach in a long time. We can have red snapper for supper tonight or shrimp or whatever your heart desires."

Relieved that he was being so compliant about it all, she felt her spirits lift. "What about shell searching? I love doing that."

He curled his arm around her waist and urged her toward the truck. "Then we'll find a whole load of them for you to take back to the ranch," he promised.

On down the bay-side street, they found a little coffee shack with outside tables, where they drank coffee and shared a danish before driving to the charter-boat place. Business there was hopping, but the personnel quickly waited on them, and in a few minutes' time, they were on board a twenty-foot cruiser with inboard motors and a covered deck.

The captain was Eric, a young man in his late twenties with jet-black hair and bronze skin. He was good-looking in a beachcomber sort of way, and in Lex's opinion, he paid entirely too much attention to Christina. But then, Lex could hardly blame the man. She was like a wild rose with her red hair flying in the wind and her blue eyes sparkling brighter than the sea itself.

Since the night of the roundup, he'd hardly been able to think of anything but her. And though he knew he was getting far too attached to her, he couldn't seem to do a damned thing to stop it. The more time he spent with her, the more he wanted.

"Can you tell us how far you think it is to the coordinates I gave you?" Christina asked Eric once they'd pulled away from the dock and headed out in the bay.

Eric answered with a pleasant smile. "Not exactly. Maybe ten, fifteen miles."

"That far?" Lex asked from a spot beneath the canopy, where he was sitting next to Christina.

"I can't be sure," Eric answered. "But I'm guessing it will be that distance."

The young captain turned his attention back to maneuvering the boat. Lex looked skeptically over at Christina. "I used to come here with Dad to fish, and I'm a bit familiar with the area. If we go that far, we'll be close to the islands."

"You're talking about Mustang and Padre?"

He nodded. "But that wouldn't make sense. If Dad fell off the boat while closer to the islands than to Corpus, then why would they bring him all the way back here for medical attention?"

For the first time since she'd met Lex, she saw suspicion flicker in his eyes, and she understood the next hour was going to be hard on him. Laying a hand over his, she said, "Let's wait and see where we are when we get there."

For the first half of the trip, the waters were full of all sorts of sailing vessels. Everything from small catamarans to commercial-sized shrimp boats to massive freighter ships could be seen bobbing atop the choppy water. But as they headed farther out to sea, only the larger vessels were visible, and they were few and far between.

Lex raised his voice to speak to the captain. "Eric, is this area normally fished?"

The young man glanced around at the open waters before looking over his shoulder at his passengers. "It depends on the time of the year and how the fish are running. Today is a slow day, but that's probably because it's Sunday morning."

Lex's attention turned to Christina, who'd been listening intently. "I suppose on a Saturday it wouldn't have been odd for my dad and his friends to be fishing this area."

Frowning, Christina nodded. "I'm still anxious to see where we'll be when we reach the right coordinates."

"So am I," Lex grimly agreed.

As the boat plowed forward into gulf waters, the wind grew stiffer, making their ride extremely rough. With his arm around Christina's shoulders, Lex kept her firmly by his side on the padded bench seat.

It was a relief when the captain finally eased off the throttle. "We're almost on top of the spot. I'll let down an anchor so you can have a better look around."

Lex was expecting to see nothing more than water. Instead, it was a shock to see land lying in front of them and less than a minute or two away.

As he and Christina rose to their feet, she asked the captain, "What's that island to the south of us?"

"That's Mustang Island. Port Aransas is about five miles to the east of us."

Lex felt as though someone had whacked the air from his lungs, and he found himself gripping Christina's hand. "Five miles, Christina! Five miles from land. Why didn't they go there instead of turning around and heading back to Corpus? It doesn't make sense! Why didn't the police question them about this?"

"They did. It's in the report. But apparently, the police decided the men had been too shaken to make clearheaded choices."

Lex couldn't stop a frustrated groan from rumbling up from his chest. "That's damned idiotic!"

"People do strange things when they're in shock, Lex." She turned her attention back to the captain. "Do you know if there are any medical services on the island? Or law officers?"

"Yeah, sure," Eric answered. "It's a state park. They have people around to take care of medical emergencies and other problems."

Lex could see the questions running through Christina's mind were the same as the ones running through his.

"Twelve years is a long time. Maybe the islands didn't

have any of those services back then," he suggested. Yet even as he said the words, Lex knew it was a far-fetched notion. It was clear that Port Aransas and medical help would have been much closer for his father than the long trip back to Corpus.

"That's something I definitely intend to research," she told him.

After a couple more minutes, Christina informed Eric that they'd seen enough, and the young captain headed the cruiser back toward the mainland. If anything, the waters had gotten rougher during their excursion, forcing her to hold on tightly to Lex's arm to keep her body from being tossed to the deck.

By the time they reached Corpus, a gray line of squall clouds had spread across the city. The two of them quickly climbed into Lex's truck and were on the verge of leaving the charter-boat service when a deluge, complete with ragged streaks of lightning bolting all the way to the ground, hit the parking lot.

"I don't see any point in getting out on the street in this stuff," Lex said. He started the engine and turned the wipers on high, but the swipes didn't come close to clearing the windshield of the tropical downpour. "The rain will probably let up in a few minutes."

"Okay by me," she said. "Looks like we got back just in time. Otherwise, we could have been toasted by lightning."

"Yeah, I don't know which is worse, being caught out on the water during a storm or caught on a horse. They both draw electricity." He turned on the air conditioner to stir the stifling air inside the vehicle. "A few years ago, we were out on spring roundup when lightning knocked one of the wranglers and his horse to the ground. He wasn't breathing when we reached him. Thankfully, Nicci happened to be riding with us that time, and she performed CPR to revive him. Later, she explained that the jolt had stopped his heart."

"Did the man have any lasting effects?"

"No. But the horse did. It frazzled his nerves. The slightest bit of sound would make him go crazy. Matt wanted to sell him after that. He feared the animal would end up injuring someone, but Cordero, Matt's brother refused to let that happen. He said all of us, even animals, need time to heal. He took the horse to Louisiana with him, and now he's right as rain."

"We all need time to heal," Christina repeated softly. "Yeah. I think your cousin is right about that." She turned an empathetic expression on him. "I know the trip we just took was hard on you, Lex."

He reached across the seat and clasped her hand in his. "It wasn't something I'd want to repeat. But I'm glad we went. Seeing that place opened my eyes to a lot of things, Christina. The accident happened closer to landmass than we'd first thought. Still, the men admitted to the police that they were frazzled. And who knows, under that sort of shock I might have used bad judgment, too."

"Geraldine knew your father inside out, and she had an innate feeling that something was wrong. We just don't know what that something was."

Christina had hardly gotten the words out when a bolt of lightning struck close behind them. She jerked with fright, and he tightened his fingers around hers. As Lex held on to her hand, he felt something inside him softening, and he ached to simply put his arm around her and nestle her head on his shoulder the way she had when Eduardo had sung about the gypsy Davey. The gentle urge was like nothing he'd felt before and it filled him with an achingly sweet wonder.

Thankfully, before he could allow himself to get too sentimental, the rain let up as abruptly as it had started. He used this as an excuse to drop her hand and reach for the gearshift.

"Let's go get a hotel room," he said in a strained, husky voice.

As he steered the truck onto the street, Christina reached over and touched his arm. "Uh, Lex—I'd better say something right now."

He darted a glance at her. "What?"

"We need to get two rooms," she said awkwardly. "One for me. One for you."

Lex pressed down on the accelerator while telling himself he wasn't disappointed. "I wasn't expecting anything else, Christina."

Five minutes later, they entered a beachside hotel and took adjoining rooms overlooking the bay.

As they rode the elevator up to the fifth floor, Lex edged closer to Christina's shoulder. "We look ridiculous getting two rooms and not carrying one bag or piece of luggage between us. I'm sure the staff behind the counter thinks we've rented two rooms just for appearances' sake."

Lifting her chin, she glanced away from him. She couldn't let him see just how easy it would be for him to seduce her into sharing one room. One bed. "I don't care what the staff thinks, or anyone else for that matter," she said stiffly.

They stepped off the elevator without exchanging any more words and found their rooms at the end of the hallway. With her entry card already in hand, Christina quickly opened the door that matched her number.

"Christina?"

His hand came down on her shoulder, and with her heart hammering, she paused to look up at him.

"Are you angry with me?" he asked.

The innocent, almost puzzled expression on his face was so endearing that she felt everything inside her melting.

"No. Why do you ask?"

"I'm not sure. A minute ago in the elevator, you sounded a little sharp."

Dropping her head, she stared at the carpet. "I didn't mean to, Lex. I knew you were only teasing."

"Look, Christina, this trip," he said lowly, then shook his head. "The reason for this trip today is not easy for me to deal with. If I seem to be making a joke at the wrong time, it's only because I—need to lighten things up. Can you understand?"

How could it be, she wondered, that he could so easily touch her heart with just a handful of words? It was scary what this man could do to her.

"Yes," she said, her throat tight. "And if I seem stiff, maybe it's because the reason for this trip is difficult for me, too. These past days, I feel as though I've gotten to know Paul personally. It bothered me to see the place where he died." Lifting her head, she looked at him and smiled. "Let's forget all this and enjoy the rest of the evening."

A smile spread across his face, and like an idiot, she felt her heart dancing at the sight. She didn't want to ask herself why this man's happiness was so important to her. For right now, it was enough that they were together.

"I'm all for that," he agreed. "After we check out our rooms, let's go down to the beach. I think the rain is all gone now."

"Give me five minutes and I'll be ready," she told him.

A short time later, Christina emerged from her room to find Lex standing in the hallway, with a cell phone to his ear. The moment he spotted her, he ended the call and slipped the small instrument back into his jeans pocket.

"I was letting Cook know that we won't be returning to the ranch tonight," he told her. "She says we're not missing a thing. It's raining cats and dogs up there now."

"I'm glad you called her. She would have been worried when we didn't show up this evening." Christina glanced wryly down at her flower-printed white dress. "Well, I'm not exactly clothed for beachcombing, but this will have to do."

Curling his arm around the back of her waist, Lex urged her down the hallway, toward the elevator doors. "Don't worry. If you get your dress dirty, I'll buy you another one."

None of her boyfriends had told Christina such a thing before, but then she'd never known a man like Lex before. She could only wonder how she would ever be able to forget him once she left the Sandbur for good.

When they reached the beach, the sun was beginning to dip low behind the skyline of the city. The wind was whipping the rolling waves, tossing Christina's red curls wildly about her face. The brown sand was damp and packed from the earlier rainstorm. She pulled off her sandals and Lex carried them for her as they strolled leisurely along the surf's edge.

"It's beautiful here," Christina said, with a wistful sigh. "Makes me realize just how long it's been since I've taken a walk on the beach. Far too long."

"It's been a long time for me, too," he replied. "I get so caught up in the ranch, the auctions, buying and selling cattle. I forget that there are other things out in the world. What about you? What reason do you have for not visiting the coastline?"

"The same reasons, I suppose. My work." She bent down and brushed the sand away from the edge of a shell. A sand dollar emerged, and though one side of the fragile sea urchin had crumbled away, she picked it up, anyway.

Lex gestured toward the shell resting in the middle of her palm. "No need for you to keep a broken shell, Christina. You'll probably find a whole one farther on down the beach."

A faint smile touched her lips. "Sometimes a person can miss out on a lot while he's searching for perfection. I think I'll keep this one."

Lex watched her fingers close around the sand dollar and wondered if he was one of those misguided persons she was talking about. From the time he'd been old enough to think about girls and the role they would play in his life, he'd decided that he'd find the perfect woman to fall in love with. His parents' marriage had been one of those rare relationships that seemed complete and happy in every way. He wanted that same sort of union for himself. But he'd never fallen in love or found that perfect woman. Maybe Christina was right. Perfection was hard to find. Or maybe he was just beginning to recognize what was perfect for him?

For a moment, an uncharacteristic stab of melancholy struck him, but he thrust it away as he curled his arm around the back of Christina's waist and smiled down at her.

"I see a restaurant on down the beach. Are you ready for some snapper?"

"Sure. Maybe you'll find that perfect shell before we get there," she impishly suggested.

"For you?"

She shook her head. "For yourself. I've already found mine."

They ate their meal of seafood on a screened-in deck overlooking the beach. Throughout the dinner, Christina was vaguely aware of the seagulls and pelicans diving and swooping over the rolling surf, of the soft music drifting from the main section of the restaurant and the delicious food melting in her mouth. Yet none of those distractions could compete with Lex.

His presence across the small wooden table was consuming her senses, and she found it almost impossible to keep her eyes off him. The moment she'd first met him, his image had practically paralyzed her with its raw sexuality. But now that she was beginning to know the hardworking, family-loving man, he was even more attractive, more of a pull on her heartstrings. And that was beginning to worry her very much. She wasn't supposed to be liking the man or his company this much.

"Looks like we're going to have a long walk in the dark," Christina remarked as she forced her eyes away from him and out toward the bay.

"So there's no reason for us not to stay and have dessert," he replied. "Thirty minutes from now, it won't be any darker."

Placing her fork on the table, she looked at him with disbelief. "Dessert! I'm too full of fish and shrimp to eat a bite of dessert!"

He grinned. "Okay. You can watch me."

He motioned to a nearby waitress, and after the young woman had given him a verbal rundown of the desserts the restaurant had to offer, he ordered some sort of chocolate concoction and coffee for both of them.

"Cook has you totally spoiled," she teased.

"She does," he admitted. "She's spoiled all of us down through the years."

"What are you going to do when she's gone?"

He looked at her sharply. "I refuse to think about that day."

"But one day she'll be too old to work for hours in the kitchen," Christina pointed out.

His gaze dropped to his plate, as though he didn't want her to see she'd discovered a soft spot in him. "I don't want to think about that, either. She's stalwart. She was on the Sandbur before I was even born, and I grew up thinking of her as a second mama. Some of my earliest memories are of standing next to her skirt, waiting for her to hand me a cookie or bandage a cut finger. When she gets…too old to work, someone else will take over." His gaze was full of conviction when he lifted it back to hers. "But Hattie will remain in the house with us. I'll make sure of that."

Impulsively, Christina reached across the table and covered his hand with hers. "I didn't mean to upset you," she said gently. "Cook is as strong as an ox. I'm sure she'll be with you for many, many more years. And I—what I'm really thinking is that I'm very jealous of you."

His brows inched upward as he glanced around them; then he leaned toward her and grinned slyly. "I don't see any other females in here giving me the eye. How could you be jealous?"

"I didn't mean in that way, Lex." Although, she had to admit to herself that the idea of any other woman clinging to his side, pressing her lips to his was too unpleasant to consider. "I'm talking about your family. You have lots of relatives living close by, plus people like Cook who are part of the Sandbur, too, and you all love and support each other. I—well, I can't imagine how nice that must be."

His thumb slipped from beneath her fingers and curled over the top of her hand. "It's not always a perfect situation, Christina. Sometimes there are arguments between us. And we often have opposing ideas on how to run the ranch. But you are right. It is nice to have family all around me. To know they'll be there if I truly need them. That's something that money can't buy."

A chill brushed across her, and she shivered slightly. "You're so right. If money could bring Joel back, I would have found him years ago."

His expression turned to one of interest. "I'm curious about your parents, Christina. What did they do when Joel went missing? Did they search for him? Were they torn up, or did they think he'd come back after a few days of partying?"

Just as she started to answer, the waitress returned with Lex's dessert, a gooey-looking brownie topped with ice cream. After she'd served them each a cup of coffee and left the table, Christina replied, "Actually, Dad had to sober up to even realize that Joel was gone. And Mom, well, she kept saying her son had just gone off on some jaunt with a friend and would be back when he got good and ready."

Lex dug his spoon into the rich sweet. "But you weren't thinking that way."

Christina thoughtfully stirred cream into her coffee. "No. Joel was very responsible. At least, he was with me. We lived together at the time. I was only twenty-one. He was eighteen. We were both in college and had moved out of the family home. Joel and I wanted to be independent. And we tried to take care of each other. God knows, we couldn't depend on our parents. They supplied us with money, but little more. By the time Joel disappeared, they'd already been divorced for eight years."

His gaze studied her face for long moments. "So when your brother went missing, your parents weren't too worried about their son?"

"No. It wasn't until a week passed that Dad decided something was wrong and launched an investigation of his own. He and Mom both hired private investigators to search for Joel, but nothing ever came from it. The few leads that came into the police department never led anywhere. It was like Joel was home one day, and the next he'd completely vanished."

Shaking his head with dismay, he said, "What was your brother like? Were you two close?"

Cradling her coffee cup in one hand, Christina used the other hand to push her tumbled hair away from her face. Other than her friend Olivia, no one ever mentioned Joel to her. Even her own parents had pushed him to the distant past. And as for Mike, she didn't think he'd ever really cared that her brother couldn't be accounted for. To have Lex express real interest about Joel touched her in a way that was impossible to describe.

"Quiet, but humorous at times. He was planning on becoming a doctor. He was brilliant with math and science, and learning came easy for him. He didn't have a steady girlfriend, but he dated frequently. He was particular about his friends and he—"

"What?" Lex prompted.

She frowned. "He literally hated our parents' behavior. Hated the way they'd hacked up their marriage—the way they'd ignored the two of us. His relationship with them was worse than strained. But he loved me. That much I never doubted."

Christina watched a thoughtful crease build in the middle of his forehead. "Do you think he might have simply walked away? That he wanted to cut himself completely away from your family?"

"I've asked myself that question a thousand times over. And I suppose he could have left without wanting to be found. But why would he want to hurt me in that way? Why would he have let me suffer all these years?" She shook her head. "I can't bear to think he'd be that cruel to me."

"Well, I have a feeling you'll find him someday. Probably where you least expect him to be."

There was such tenderness in his words that tears stung the back of her eyes. She looked away from him and swallowed. "Thank you for the optimism, Lex. I know it's a long shot, but I won't give up. I can't."

Several seconds slipped by in silence, and then he said, "Here. Try some of this. It's delicious."

She looked around to see that he was holding a spoonful of the chocolate dessert toward her as though it was a cure-all. Christina couldn't help but laugh.

"Lex, I'm stuffed. You eat it."

"No. I won't eat another bite until you do," he insisted.

Rolling her eyes in a good-natured way, she caved in. "All right. One bite. Just to make you happy."

"That's my girl." His eyes gleamed as she opened her mouth and leaned toward the spoon.

As Christina slipped the bite of dessert into her mouth, it felt almost decadent to have him feeding her, especially with the same spoon his lips had touched.

"Mmm. It melts right on your tongue," she told him. "You're right. It's delicious."

Sensing that things between them were changing to something far too intimate, Christina leaned back in her chair and turned her attention to her coffee. Lex continued to eat his dessert, but all the while his eyes were on her, arousing her in ways that left her feeling slightly drunk and even more reckless.

Finally, to her relief, he put down his spoon and announced, "I'm done. If you are, I'll pay us out."

There was no point in staying longer. Her coffee cup was empty, and they had to return to the hotel sooner or later.

"Yes. I'm ready whenever you are."

Lex motioned for the waitress, and in only a few minutes, they were out the door and once again walking across the beach. Lights from nearby businesses were enough to faintly illuminate the sandy pathway. Even so, Lex insisted on keeping his arm around the back of her waist.

"I don't want you to fall," he said as he urged her close to his side.

The connection to his body left her heart thumping fast and hard, making her voice sound a bit breathless. "We're walking on sand, Lex. If I fell, I'd hardly hurt myself."

"Hmm. Don't be so practical. I have to have a reason to keep my arm around you."

"Do you? Have to have a reason?"

She didn't know why those teasing words had come out of her mouth. Something about being alone with this man, away from his family and home, was doing strange things to her thinking. Or was it her body that was doing all the thinking? Either way, she couldn't resist his touch.

With a grunt of pleasure, he tugged the front of her body up against his and settled his hands at the small of her back. "It doesn't feel that way to me. Not tonight."

She started to tell him he was taking a lot for granted. But the words didn't have a chance to form on her tongue before he was lowering his head and fastening his lips over hers.

He tasted like chocolate and coffee and Lex. An utterly sinful combination and one that quickly squashed what little resistance she'd been trying to hold on to. Her mouth opened and slanted against the hard curve of his lips; her hands slipped up and linked at the back of his neck.

The strong trade winds crashed against their bodies, but they weren't nearly enough to cool the heat rushing from the soles of Christina's bare feet all the way to the roots of her hair. Unconsciously, she pressed herself closer. His eager kiss left her feeling as though he was lifting her completely off the ground.

His hands swept across her back and down the length of her spine until they reached the curved swell of her buttocks. Once there, they urged her hips forward until she was clamped tightly against his swelling manhood.

The fact that he was reacting so strongly to her and letting her know it somehow fueled her desire even more. For the next few minutes, she forgot that they were on a public beach, forgot that she was supposed to be guarding herself against this man's charms.

It wasn't until her dazed senses noted nearby voices that she was finally able to gather enough strength to pull her lips away from his and step out of his arms.

He tugged on her hand and murmured huskily, "Christina, come back here."

Unable to meet his gaze, she whispered, "Here comes a group of people. We have an audience."

Muttering an impatient curse under his breath, he started down the beach, tugging her along with him. "Don't they know this is our little strip of beach?"

"Guess they didn't see the Private—Keep Out signs," she tried to joke, but even to her own ears, her voice sounded strained and odd. Their embrace had gone far beyond just a kiss, and they both knew it. Her next question probably sounded inane, but she asked it, anyway. "Where are we going now?"

He glanced down at her, and she was surprised to see there was no sexy, teasing grin on his face. Instead, his expression was quietly serious as his gaze intently probed hers.

"To the hotel. To my room. Are you…agreeable to that?"

All she had to do was say one little word and everything would stay the same. She'd wake up in the morning with her world safely on its axis. But the night ahead would be cold and empty. Just like the nights of the past three years, since she'd walked away from Mike, had been.

"Lex, I—"

With a hand on her shoulder, he stopped her forward progress long enough to plant a kiss on her cheek. "Don't spoil this night by thinking too much, Christina. I want you and you want me. That's enough for now, isn't it?"

It had to be, Christina thought. Because she couldn't seem to stop him from leading her wherever he wanted to go.

She silently nodded, and they walked the rest of the way to the hotel without exchanging another word.

Chapter Seven

Inside the hotel, they went straight to the elevator, and once the doors cocooned them inside the small, private space, Lex used the opportunity to pull her back into his arms and kiss her.

The contact, though brief, was enough to overwhelm her all over again, and she was barely aware of her surroundings when they left the elevator and walked down the quiet hallway to his room.

The nicely furnished space was a replica of hers, but unlike her, he'd left the drapes pulled back on the glass doors leading out to the balcony. Beyond, stars were hanging over the gulf waters, sparkling the beach with diamonds.

With the door shut behind them, Lex took her by the hand and led her over to the sliding glass doors. "Let's step out on the balcony," he said softly, "where I can look at you in the starlight."

They stepped outside on the small balcony enclosed by black wrought iron. From this height, the wind seemed even stronger, and it whipped Christina's hair across her face as she gazed out at the rolling surf.

"It's beautiful," she said wistfully. He was standing directly behind her, and the bare skin on her shoulders was sizzling where his fingers rested. "And I'm glad we're here. Even though the reason for the trip isn't a pleasant one."

Turning her toward him, he cradled her face with his palms and lowered his lips toward hers. The idea that they were well and truly alone and about to make love made her whole body ache with anticipation.

"This trip was meant to happen, my sweet. Just like a lot of other things."

She didn't know exactly what he meant by that. But the moment his mouth touched hers, it stopped mattering. Nothing mattered but his touch.

They kissed for long moments, until the connection was no longer enough to satisfy their needs, and Lex led her gently back inside and over to the king-size bed.

With nothing but the starlight filtering through the glass doors, he found the zipper at the back of her dress and slowly pulled it downward. Christina closed her eyes and bit down on her bottom lip as his hands followed the garment down her curves, then onto the floor.

Shivering, she carefully stepped out of the pool of fabric, and he tossed it toward the armchair sitting in the corner of the room.

"Are you cold?" he whispered, with concern.

Daring to meet his gaze, she felt her heart squeeze with inexplicable pain. "No. I—I'm just not sure I—we—should be doing this. That I should be…wanting you this much."

Smiling, he rested his forehead against hers. "Hang on, baby. If this is a mistake, we'll be making it together."

This couldn't be a mistake, Christina thought moments later, as Lex gently peeled away her undergarments and lifted her onto the massive bed. Even without the touch of his hands, she was on fire for him, mindlessly needing to feel his skin, his body against her.

She waited patiently for him to shed his boots and clothing, but once he lay down next to her, she reached for him eagerly and sighed with contentment when his mouth once again came down over hers. The stroke of his hands, the hungry plunder of his lips were enough to push her senses over the edge, and soon she was writhing against him, urging him to connect their bodies.

If anything, she'd thought that Lex would be a smooth, practiced lover, that his moves would be controlled and predictable. But nothing about his ragged kisses or the shaky, erratic movements of his hands showed a man on automatic pilot. He kissed her, touched her as though each time was a new experience and he could hardly wait for the next one.

His eagerness left her breathless, her body coiled with a hunger that ached deep within her. Like a warm rain shower, he kissed her cheeks, nose, chin and eyelids. Then on a slower track, he moved his attention behind her ear and down the sensitive side of her neck.

She felt like the bud of a flower, and each time he touched her, one more petal opened to expose the very center of her being. When his lips found a nipple and pulled it deep within his mouth, she was certain she was going to break apart. A broken cry gurgled in her throat, and she wrapped her legs around his hips.

"Make love to me, Lex." She whispered the plea. "Now. Please!"

He lifted his head. "Are you—"

Guessing his question, she finished for him. "I'm protected."

Whispering her name, he touched her face with the tips of his fingers, then slid them into her thick hair. At the same time, he lowered the bottom half of his body down to hers and entered her as slowly and gently as his raging desire would allow. But once the sweet, damp folds of her womanhood enveloped him, his control crumbled.

A hot ache gripped his loins, forcing him to thrust deeply and rapidly as he searched for relief, for something inside her that would quench the flames threatening to consume him.

At some point, he became aware of her hips driving up to meet his, her open mouth exploring his chest, her tongue teasing his nipples. She felt small and fragile beneath him, yet her abandoned movements told him that she wanted everything he was giving her and more. The idea aroused him even more than the feel of her body, and before he could stop himself, he was blindly pounding into her.

Time seemed suspended as sweat slicked his body and dripped onto hers. His hands raced over her smooth ivory skin, cupped around her breasts, then finally anchored themselves at the sides of her waist.

From somewhere far away, he could hear her soft cries, the whisper of his name, but the sounds faded as his heartbeat roared louder and louder in his ears. The ragged breaths he sucked into his lungs did little to ease their fiery pain, until suddenly breathing didn't seem to matter at all. He'd been flung to paradise, and Christina had taken the journey with him.

Long, long moments passed before Christina drifted back to the quiet room, and even then her awareness returned only in increments. Everything was still spinning, but she could feel Lex's cheek resting on hers, his heart pounding against her breast, his legs tangled with hers. Sweat was stinging her eyes, while her lungs were straining to draw in another breath.

Her eyes fluttered open just as he rolled his weight off her. Groaning softly, she shifted to face him, then sighed as he reached to tuck the front of her body up against his. Her lips curved into a satisfied smile as he pressed tiny kisses across her forehead.

"It has to be a hundred degrees in here," he said.

The unexpectedness of his words deepened the smile on her face. "The air-conditioning must have gone off."

He chuckled lowly. "Or maybe all this heat is coming from the firebrand in my arms."

Feeling like more of a woman than she'd ever felt in her life, she trailed her fingers along his damp cheek. "I didn't think it would be this way with us," she said lowly.

In the dim light of the room, she could see the corners of his mouth tilt upward.

"How did you think it would be?"

In spite of the wild ride they'd just taken together, Christina could feel a blush creeping over her face. "I—I'm not sure. More reserved, I suppose."

That brought another rumbling chuckle up from the depths of his chest, and Christina realized it was a happy, soothing sound. One that made her glad to be alive.

"Honey, nothing between us will ever be lukewarm."

His hand slid slowly from her shoulder to the curve of her hip. Desire stirred deep within her, shocking her with its quick reappearance.

"And that scares me, Lex."

Groaning, he cupped his palms around the sides of her face. "Oh, Christina, nothing about this—about you and me—should scare you."

He would think that way, she thought dully. This wasn't a life-changing event for him. And she'd be naive and childish to think it could be.

Doing her best to push away the raw ache in her heart, she said, "You're right, Lex. Nothing should worry me tonight."

With a groan of pleasure, he crushed her body even closer and brought his lips to hers. Christina thought she was too exhausted to make love a second time, but Lex proved her wrong, and as the moon rose over the bay, she clung to him and wondered where this night was going to take her. And how soon it would be before her heart was broken all over again.

The next morning Christina woke at the sound of a door opening and closing. When she cracked her eyes open, sunlight smacked her in the face.

"Good morning, beautiful. Ready for some coffee?"

Rolling to her back, she saw Lex holding a paper carrier with four cups nestled safely inside it. He was already dressed in the clothes he'd worn yesterday, and when he pulled off his hat, she could see his blond hair was brushed smoothly back from his forehead. He couldn't have looked more sexy or handsome, and she felt her heart flutter like a lost leaf in the wind.

Clutching the sheet to her breasts, she quickly scooted up in the bed. "Four cups of coffee! Were you planning on jolting me awake with caffeine?"

Laughing, he sat down on the edge of the bed and placed the cups of coffee on the nightstand. "No, I wanted us to have plenty. Besides, I was going to kiss you awake before too long. I have a surprise for you."

After taking the lid off one of the foam cups, he poured in cream, then handed it to her. She thanked him, then took a careful sip of the steaming liquid. "A surprise?" she repeated groggily. "What sort of surprise?"

He left the bed and moved across the room, to where a small desk was positioned a short distance away from the balcony door. She watched with complete dismay as he lifted a shiny silver gift bag from the desktop and carry it back to the bed.

"Where on earth did that come from? A shop in the lobby? I didn't see anything last night," she said.

"The coffee came from the hotel lobby. But not this. While you've been sleeping, I've been out shopping."

"Why didn't you wake me? It's late, and we need to be getting to the bait house. You need to get back to the Sandbur and—"

He held up a hand. "Quit worrying. We'll be back to the Sandbur soon enough."

He was certainly right about that, she thought. Soon this time they'd had together would end, and she didn't have a clue what the future would bring for the two of them. Last night his pillow talk had been light and playful, and she'd taken his cue and kept hers the same. Yet deep down she was scared to death that she was falling head over heels for the man, and she didn't have the courage to even give him a hint as to how she was feeling.

Gently, he took the coffee from her hand and pushed the gift bag toward her. "See if you like it. I picked it out myself."

Christina peeked inside the bag and saw some sort of garment neatly folded at the bottom. With a cry of pleasure, she forgot about holding the sheet to her naked body and concentrated on pulling the item out in the open.

Ice-blue fabric spilled across her lap, and she quickly

discovered it was a dress fashioned from polished cotton. The waist was nipped in with a belt edged with white piping, the top was V-necked and sleeveless, while the skirt flared out in deep gores, which would swish against her calves as she walked. It was very pretty and even more sexy, and she couldn't wait to try it on.

"Oh! Oh, how sweet of you, Lex! It's beautiful! I love it!"

"I thought you'd like something fresh to put on this morning."

She couldn't believe he'd done such a thoughtful, romantic thing for her. She wanted to believe that she was the *only* woman who'd ever received this sort of treatment from him, but that was highly unlikely. From what she'd heard, the man had made a career out of women since he'd been old enough to flirt.

You knew that beforehand, Christina. So don't think about it now. Just enjoy this moment with him.

"I do," she murmured, then leaned forward and placed a soft kiss on his lips. "Thank you."

He didn't say anything. Instead, he simply touched her cheek and gazed at her as though he were watching the sun rise. Every word, every intimate touch that had passed between them last night replayed in her mind, and after a few moments, Christina was so overwhelmed with emotions that she had to clear her throat and ease back from him. Otherwise, everything she was feeling was going to be there on her face for him to read.

"I'd better shower and get dressed," she said huskily.

Wrapping the sheet around her, she scooted off the bed and headed toward the bathroom. She was about to step through the door when Lex called out to her. Glancing over her shoulder, she arched her brows at him.

"Christina, I just wanted to say—in case you're wondering—the dress wasn't meant to be any sort of...payment."

She stiffened. "I never thought it was."

Suddenly he was across the room, reaching for her hand and drawing the back of it to his lips. "Forgive me, Christina, if that sounded coarse. I—I know you think I do this sort of thing often. That I go through women the way I buy and sell cattle. But that's far from the truth. And if I'm not doing any of this right, well—" One corner of his mouth turned upward in a hapless grin. "I've just ruined the hell out of my reputation."

Softly, she touched her fingers to his cheek. "Lex, you bought me the dress because you wanted me to have it. You were being sweet and thoughtful and nothing more."

Relief flooded his expression. "You're a special woman," he murmured.

Was being special the same as being loved? she wondered dismally. No. She didn't think so. But being special to a man like Lex was probably the most she could ever hope for.

Tears suddenly stung the back of her eyes.

"I'll be ready in a few minutes," she told him, then hurriedly shut the bathroom door between them.

A half hour later, after checking out of the hotel and grabbing a bite of breakfast at a seaside grill, Lex drove the two of them back to Ray's Bait.

Unlike yesterday, the bait shop was busy with several customers. Christina and Lex waited to one side until the store emptied and the stocky man behind the counter was alone. Then they stepped up to introduce themselves.

Ray Pena had salt-and-pepper hair, a broad face, a thick neck and shoulders and enormous hands to match. A faded tropical shirt was stretched tightly across his belly. He smiled affably at the two of them before settling his appreciative gaze back on Christina.

"You two don't look like you're goin' fishin' today. What can I do for you?"

At least the man was observant, Christina thought, with a measure of hope. "You're right. We're not here to buy bait. I don't know if your assistant told you or not, but we stopped by yesterday, when you were out."

Ray Pena grimaced. "No. Sally don't tell me much. 'Cept she don't make enough money." He snorted. "Young people nowadays think they deserve a raise just for showin' up." His squinted gaze vacillated between Christina and Lex. "You folks work for the Texas Rangers or somethin'?"

Christina could see how the man might take Lex for a Ranger. Lex had that solid, authoritative look about him. As for her, there was no way this man could know that she'd put in five years with that organization. "No. I'm a private investigator and—" she glanced over to Lex "—he's my client. If you have a minute, we'd like to show you some photos and ask you a few questions."

Ray shrugged. "Sure. Ain't got no customers now, anyway."

Christina stepped closer to the counter, while Lex moved up behind her left shoulder. Instantly, she was aware of his body heat, the faint scent of masculine cologne lingering on his clothing. His nearness was more than a distraction, but she forced her mind to focus on one of the few witnesses that had seen Paul Saddler the day he died.

"This is about a drowning that happened close to twelve years ago," she explained to Ray Pena. "Some businessmen bought bait in your shop, then went out in the gulf for a day of fishing. One of them didn't return to Corpus alive."

Ray's broad face wrinkled into a thoughtful grimace. "Ma'am, people drown in the gulf all the time. Never think the water is a danger until it's too late."

Christina glanced up to Lex, and he flashed her a hopeless look. Determined, she pulled a packet of photos from a manila envelope in her handbag and spread them across the glass counter. "Well, you might remember this event because the police came around to question you about that day. You see, there was an inquiry about the way this man died. His name was Paul Saddler. He was a prominent rancher from the Sandbur and a businessman for Coastal Oil."

"Hmm, sounds familiar. Let me see."

He fetched a pair of reading glasses from his shirt pocket and, after jamming them on his face, leaned over the photos. The snapshots had been taken at a Coastal Oil Christmas party and saved along with many of Paul's papers. Christina had considered it lucky to find photos for which all four men had posed together, with their faces in full view of the camera.

"Yeah, yeah," Ray said after a quick study of the photos. He tapped a finger on Paul's image. "I remember this was the man who drowned. The story was all over the papers and on the TV news."

"So you remember that day?" Christina eagerly prompted.

"Sure." He turned around and poured himself a cup full of burned coffee. As he added a hefty measure of sugar, he went on, "Before the drowning, those guys had come in here pretty regular. I was always happy to see 'em 'cause they usually spent a lot of money."

Christina left the photos where they lay. "Do you recall the day of the drowning?"

"Damn right. I heard the emergency call come over the police scanner. I used to listen to one of those all the time, but the damn thing got struck by lightning and I never got another one. The old lady was afraid if it happened again, it might burn the whole place down."

Christina waited patiently while he took a long swig of the coffee. "So when you heard the police call, you recognized Paul Saddler's name?" she asked.

Ray shook his head. "Nope. Before that, I didn't know any of their names. They were just customers, you know. Guys that would shoot the bull while waiting for me to sack up their bait. I didn't know it was him that had drowned until I saw his picture in the paper the next day. Hit me hard. Knowin' that I'd been talking to him that mornin' and a few hours later he was dead."

Christina looked up at Lex again. This time his expression was grim. She thrust her hand behind her until she found his fingers and latched hers tightly around them.

"Yes, I know exactly what you mean," Christina told Ray. "So, can you tell me anything about that particular visit from the men that day? Did anything seem unusual with any of them?"

Ray pointed to Red Winters. "The big redhead was loud. But he was always like that—tellin' crude jokes and ordering the other guys around—kinda teasin' like, you know, but obnoxious. That day, the thin man with the glasses barked at him in a testy way. Surprised the hell out of me. He never showed much spunk."

"What about Paul? Was anything different about him?"

Ray thought for long moments, and as they waited for him to answer, she could feel Lex's fingers tightening around hers even more. At that moment, Christina realized how very much she wanted to solve this case for Lex's sake. He'd loved his father deeply, and he deserved to know the truth about his death.

"Come to think of it, I seem to recall I told the cops that he was real quiet that mornin'. Didn't talk much at all and stood off by himself most of the time. I thought he might be sick. He sorta looked it."

"What made you think that?" Christina questioned. Being sick and being nervous could produce the same outward symptoms. "Was he coughing? Running to the restroom? Anything like that?"

Ray shook his head. "Not as I remember. He just looked pale and like he wasn't havin' a good time. But who could have enjoyed a fishin' trip with that redheaded bastard? He's the one who needed to go overboard. The guy that drowned—now, he was a class act. Always nice and friendly. I hated hearin' that he was dead. Really hated it. He treated me like an equal, you know? The others—they were different."

Christina knew all too well what Ray Pena meant, and she was beginning to get a whole new picture of Paul Saddler's coworkers.

"So after Paul's death, did the other three men ever show up here at the bait house again?"

"Once. Not the skinny man with the glasses. But the other two stopped by not long after the drowning. The redhead was real surly, and I was about to order him to leave when the other guy—the pretty boy—got him and took him out to the parking lot. I think the both of them might have been a little drunk, but since they left without causing any trouble, I didn't call the cops."

"And they never came back after that?" Lex asked.

"No," Ray replied. "Guess their friend's death must have taken the enjoyment out of fishin'."

Christina returned the photos to the manila envelope. After she stuffed it back into her handbag, she reached across the counter to shake the shop owner's hand. "Thank you very much, Mr. Pena. You've been more helpful than you can imagine."

After Lex also shook the man's hand and offered his appreciation for the information, they turned to leave the bait house, but Ray had a question of his own that caused the two of them to pause at the door.

"What's this all about, anyway? Y'all think Paul Saddler was murdered or somethin'?"

"We're looking into every possibility," Christina told him.

"Seems like a long time ago to be worryin' about it now," Ray muttered, more to himself than to them.

They left the bait house and climbed back into the truck. As Christina fastened her seat belt and Lex started the engine, he said, "I could tell by the way Ray Pena talked about Red that he remembered the group of men and the day Dad died. That surprised me."

"When a tragedy occurs, it usually sparks a person's memory." Crossing her legs, she turned toward him. "His recollection of Lawrence Carter barking at Red was the thing that caught my attention. Would you say that behavior was out of character for Lawrence?"

Lex nodded as he steered the car onto a major boulevard. "It surprised the hell out of me, too. I never knew Lawrence to say a sharp word to anyone. But everybody can reach a breaking point, and that morning, Red might have been getting on Lawrence's nerves."

Ideas about how the tragedy happened were slowly beginning to form in Christina's mind. Still, there were pieces of the puzzle that still needed to be found. That meant gathering more information and more time spent on the Sandbur.

The idea left her torn. Every fiber of her being wanted to be near Lex, to make love to him any and every chance she got. But the sensible part of her brain knew that would be a dangerous gamble and the stakes would be her heart.

"You look extra beautiful this morning," Lex commented, breaking the short silence. "Must be that pretty dress."

Glancing down, she smoothed a hand across her lap. "You have very good taste."

"I know."

The suggestive lilt to his words had her glancing up to see his wicked gaze traveling up and down the length of her. The look caused desire to simmer in the pit of her stomach, yet at the same time, she was chilled with fear, terrified each hour, each day in his company would only make her fall in love with the man just that much more.

"Lex…about last night. I think—"

Her words halted as he reached across the console and folded his hand around hers.

"Last night was something I'll never forget," he said gently.

She drew in a shaky breath. "Neither will I."

From the corner of her eye, she could see him glance at her, and for a split second, she thought she saw genuine affection on his face. Would she be crazy to think he might want more from her than just sex?

"Is something wrong? You look a little sad."

Shrugging, she prayed he couldn't see the turmoil inside of her. "I wish…we could have stayed here at the beach a bit longer."

A smug smile spread across his face. "Don't worry, honey. I'll come up with a reason for us to make another trip down here. And soon."

That was exactly what Christina was afraid of. One more repeat of last night and she'd be totally lost to the man.

Chapter Eight

As soon as Lex and Christina returned to the ranch, he was caught up in business. A cattle buyer from New Mexico was already there, waiting for him to arrive. Later that day, he had to drive out to the Mission River Division of the ranch, where the hands were cutting more cattle to be sent to market. Tuesday was taken up entirely with a trip with Matt to a cattle breeders convention in Austin. By the time he'd returned home, Christina had already retired for the night, and Lex had gone to bed frustrated. Since their time in Corpus, he'd not had a chance to spend five minutes with her, and they'd only spoken briefly a few times on the phone.

But that didn't mean Lex had forgotten one moment of their time together. Just the memory of having her in his arms left him aroused and desperate to make love to her again.

Make love. Make love. Why are you thinking in those terms, Lex? Have you fallen in love with Christina?

The question jolted him. He'd never been in love before. Infatuated maybe, but not the deep sort of love that burrowed into a person's heart and stayed there. If he was in love with Christina, he wasn't sure what or how he was supposed to feel. He only knew that being with Christina, in any capacity, had become very important to him. He knew he didn't want this time with her to end.

So what was he going to do about it? The questions continued to gnaw at him as he made his way to the small room where Christina had set up her office, yet he did his best to push them aside as he knocked on the open door and stepped over the threshold.

"Good morning, stranger," he greeted, with a grin. "Cook told me you already had breakfast and were here working. You've started early."

Snapping her cell phone together, she laid the instrument aside and gave him a halfhearted smile. "Your father must have kept everything he ever worked on. I still haven't made it through all these folders."

Even though she looked as gorgeous as ever in a pale pink blouse and a dove-gray miniskirt, he could sense a change in her, and he wondered what could have happened with her these past days he'd been away from the ranch house.

"If my memory is right, I believe there are even more of Dad's things in the attic." He gestured toward the boxes stacked near her desk. "Have you found anything helpful here?"

"I've come across a few interesting notes about the company shares and an e-mail from Red to Paul, urging him to buy more shares, saying that he had a solid tip the value was going to go up."

Lex stepped closer to where she sat. "When was the message dated?"

Christina glanced at a legal pad lying on the corner of the desk. “About a year before Paul died.”

Shrugging, Lex said, “Well, that’s nothing suspicious. It was a well-known fact that Coastal was hatching an enormous venture at the time. A trans-state pipeline that would supply several states with natural gas. If everything had gone as planned, the project would have made Coastal billions of dollars. But state legislation began to bog things down, and then a big backer got cold feet. When the idea was shelved, Coastal’s stock plummeted, and it took nearly a decade for it to climb back to its former worth.”

Christina’s brows arched with interest. “What about your father’s shares? I’ve not come across any sort of documents showing that he sold them.”

Lex shook his head. “He kept them. And then Mom hung on to the stock through all those thin years. Dad had always voiced his confidence in the company, so Mom figured she should trust his judgment. Turned out he was correct. She still has the stock, and it’s now worth a small fortune.”

“Hmm.” Christina thoughtfully tapped a pencil against the legal pad, then she rose from the chair and walked around the desk to stand near him. Lex felt like a weak fool as his heart began to thump at a high rate of speed. What was it about this woman that affected him so? he wondered. The exotic scent she wore? Her smooth, luscious skin, the curves hidden beneath her clothing? Or was it her eyes and the way she looked at him? The way they darkened and lightened to her moods, the way her lips tilted when she smiled at him? God, he wished he knew, because he felt as though he was losing control of his own life.

“I’m not yet ready to say. I still need to do a lot more digging.” Her blue eyes connected with his. “And I’m glad you came by this morning. I needed to let you know that I'm planning another trip."

An eager grin flashed across his face. "For us?"

Her gaze darted uncomfortably away from his, underscoring his earlier suspicion that something had changed with her. Now he could only wait, like a horse thief waiting for the trapdoor to fall from beneath his feet. What made her put up this invisible wall between them? He'd thought making love would move their relationship forward, not back.

She drew in a deep breath and blew it out. "No. I'm driving up to San Antonio tomorrow. Alone. I have several things to do."

It was crazy how disappointed he felt. He'd never dreamed that any woman could make him feel *this* much. And he couldn't stop himself from reaching for her. As soon as his hands came down on her shoulders, her eyes turned misty, and the sight tore a hole right in the middle of his chest.

"I thought…I was hoping you'd want me to go along," he murmured.

She closed her eyes, as though his question pained her. "I've been thinking about that, Lex. About Corpus—"

Hearing the misgivings in her voice, he interrupted her with a loud groan. "Oh hell, Christina, don't tell me you've been having second thoughts about our night together."

He crossed the room and carefully shut the door, cocooning them in the private office. His mother was away on a business trip, but he didn't want any of the maids coming by and disturbing them.

With a helpless shake of her head, she pressed the heel of her palm against her forehead. "Oh, Lex. I don't regret it. Or—well, maybe I do, a bit. Because—" Her gaze dropped from his. "I think I've sent you the wrong signals."

"Signals?" he repeated as he walked back over to her. "What are you talking about?"

Her head lifted, and the misery he saw in her eyes tore at him. He didn't want to hurt this woman. More than anything, he wanted to make her happy.

"I made it look as though I was willing to have an affair with you. And I shouldn't have done that. Because I'm—I can't have that sort of relationship in my life again. It would be wrong for me, and you."

His nostrils flared as unexpected pain plowed through him. She wanted to write him off. Without even giving him a chance. Giving the two of them a chance.

"Christina, why did you go to bed with me?"

She swallowed hard as her eyes turned watery.

"I'm only human, Lex. I wanted you. And I told myself that I could deal with having casual sex with you."

In his past, Lex would probably have been relieved to hear a woman describing their time together as casual. But he wasn't now. He felt offended and even a bit crushed. And the fact only pointed out to him just how much he'd changed since he'd met Christina.

"Christina, nothing about that night—our night together—was casual. And you know it!"

She looked anguished. "Oh please, Lex. You've never talked about looking for a permanent woman in your life. So don't pretend with me now. That would—that would make everything worse."

Stepping forward, he reached for her hand and pressed it between his palms. "I haven't been looking for a permanent woman, because I gave up on that idea. This love thing just never happened for me! Still, that doesn't mean I don't care about you. About us being together."

Like heavy stones, disappointment fell to the bottom of her heart. Caring was nothing like loving. He wanted their bodies to be connected, but not their hearts. "Is that supposed to be enough for me?"

"I'm not going to pretend with you, Christina. That's not my style. We have a good thing going between us. I don't know where it's going, but I'd like to find out."

The smoldering look in his eyes warned her that he was about to kiss her, and Christina knew she was in far too vulnerable a state to let that happen. One taste of his lips and she'd be promising him anything.

Sighing, she pulled her hand from his and walked over to a window that overlooked the lawn. He followed, and as he came to a stop behind her, his hands lapped over her shoulders, branding her with tempting heat.

"Christina, the only way we can get to know each other is to *be* together."

The ache of frustration caused her to close her eyes and pinch the bridge of her nose. "Oh, Lex, Mother admitted that the only thing that had drawn her to Dad in the first place was sex. I've never wanted to follow in her footsteps. But now I'm beginning to wonder if something in me is just as weak as her."

"Listen, honey," he said gently, "making love to me hardly makes you a duplicate of your mother."

Turning, she looked up at him, and as she did, she realized his face had become a dear image in her heart. It was something she wanted, needed to look upon every day of her life.

"Lex, I think you need to know that I spent four years in a relationship with a fellow law officer. His name was Mike, and I thought—well, I believed—he loved me. He certainly told me that often enough. But they were just empty words.

Just like his promises of marriage. It took me a long time to realize that I was wasting my time with the man and a whole lot of willpower to finally pack up and leave."

He was clearly surprised, and she wondered what he was thinking of her now. That maybe she was a woman who couldn't hold on to a lasting relationship?

"Four years," he repeated. "That's a long time. You must have loved the man."

Glancing away from him, she swallowed as emotion filled her throat. Now that she'd met Lex, it was plain that she'd never loved Mike. Not the eternal kind that outlives good times, bad times, old age and even death. With Mike, she'd simply loved the idea of being a wife, having children and a family of her own. There was a wealth of difference.

"I'm not sure I knew what love was back then. But at the time I believed that I loved him. Otherwise, I wouldn't have lived with him."

His eyes widened, and she realized she'd surprised him even more. But she couldn't worry about how he was viewing her now. He needed to understand where she was coming from and where she intended to go. She wasn't going to make the same mistake with him that she'd made with Mike. Living on hope was no longer enough for her.

"You lived with him?"

Christina nodded. "Does that shock you?"

His head wagged back and forth. "Well—uh, it shakes me more than anything. When you told me that you'd come close to marriage, I thought you'd probably just worn some guy's engagement ring for a few months. Living together is—that's commitment."

"Not to him," she said dully.

Before he could reply, she walked over to her desk and

sank into the leather chair. The small space she'd put between them wasn't enough to ease the trembling inside of her, the ache to rush back to him and fling her arms around his neck.

Looping his thumbs over his belt, Lex moved in front of the desk and stared directly into her blue eyes. It amazed her that she didn't see revulsion or disappointment in his eyes. Especially knowing how he admired his parents' relationship and wanted that same sort of relationship for himself. She was far, far from being a flawless human being.

"All right, Christina. I've listened to what you've had to say. Now listen to me. And I'm going to put this in simple terms. I'm not the playboy some people think I am. And I'm not like this Mike you once—knew."

Fighting back tears, she said, "It's wrong of you to ask me to jump into a heated physical relationship with you, Lex! We need to get to know each other better before we make such a serious connection."

For long moments, his gaze searched her face, and Christina suspected he was searching for a gentlemanly way to end things between them. But he surprised her when he finally spoke.

"All right, Christina. For now, we'll do this thing your way. We'll go slow and get to know each other better. But just remember that all the while, I'll be wanting to make love to you. And you'll be wanting to make love to me. We'll be wasting time when we could be making each other happy."

Maybe he was right, she thought dismally. But her feelings for him had become too important. She needed to know whether the caring he felt for her had a chance at turning into love, or if his desire for her would quickly burn itself out.

Rising from the chair, she walked around to where he stood and placed a whisper-soft kiss on his cheek. The tiny expression of affection couldn't begin to describe the gratitude swelling in her heart. "I know you're not happy with me about this, Lex. But I'm glad you're willing—for now—to go along with my wishes."

She eased back from him before her arms could turn traitorous and fling themselves around his neck.

With a reluctant grin, he rubbed the spot she'd just kissed. "One of these days—and soon—you'll be planting a kiss on my lips instead of my cheek. But only when you're ready. I promise you that," he murmured huskily. Then, before she could guess his intentions, he lifted the back of her hand to his lips and took his time pressing a kiss against the soft skin. "So, why are you going to San Antone this time? Another case, or Dad's?"

Relieved that he'd changed the subject, she said, "Your father's. I'm going to try again to catch up to Paul's old friends. I want to hear with my own ears how they recount the day your father died."

Worry chased everything else from his face, and he quickly clasped both her hands between his. "Christina, we're not entirely sure these guys were being truthful about Dad's accident! That puts them all under suspicion! I don't like the idea of you seeing them. Not one bit."

"I have to interview them in person, Lex. That way, I can see if they're hiding something. And more than anything, I need to catch them off guard."

"I can understand that. But if these guys actually did have anything to do with Dad's death, they might be dangerous. Especially to you, since you're digging open the case."

Did his show of concern mean anything? she wondered. Only minutes ago he'd admitted that he cared for her, but did that sort of caring warrant this much worry?

Don't let yourself start believing the man actually loves you, Christina. He's already said that heartfelt emotion wasn't for him. Remember that.

Emotions knotted her throat, making her voice husky when she spoke. "You're forgetting, Lex, that I worked as a law officer for several years. I know the danger signs to look for, and I know how to be careful. Besides, this is what your mother hired me to do."

The scowl on his face said her words hadn't assured him all that much. She had to remind herself that if he was the one putting himself in danger, she wouldn't like it. In fact, she wanted to make sure, before this was all over with, that he didn't get anywhere near Paul's old friends.

Tossing his hands up in a helpless gesture, he said, "Well, I can't tell you how to do your job. Just like you couldn't tell me how to go out and rope a wild bull that might gore me or my horse to death."

The image of his words sent a shiver down Christina's spine. City folks like her never stopped to appreciate the constant dangers of a cowboy's life. Everything about Lex was opening her eyes. And her heart. But what good was that going to do her if his own heart was closed to love?

"I'll be very careful, Lex. I promise." Then before she could stop herself, she gave into the overwhelming need to touch him. She stepped closer and lifted her mouth to his. He instantly took the initiative, and for long moments, his lips searched and coaxed until she was moaning deep in her throat and wrapping her arms around his waist.

By the time he finally lifted his head, Christina's cheeks were on fire. One more minute and her vow to resist him would have crumbled. The worst part was the smug grin on his face that said he knew she'd been on the verge of melting.

"When I said you'd soon be kissing me on the lips, I didn't realize it was going to be in a matter of minutes."

"That was a goodbye kiss," she said, with as much dignity as she could muster.

His chuckle matched the sexy glint in his eyes. "I can't wait to see what your hello is going to be like when you return."

Turning her back to him, she bit down on her lip and blinked at the mist in her eyes. She wasn't like Retha Logan. She wasn't even that same young woman who fell victim to Mike's charming lies, she told herself. But, oh, it was going to be very lonely while proving that to Lex. And herself.

Three days later, on her way from San Antonio back to the Sandbur, Christina drove to the riverside area where Olivia's law firm and Christina's own working office were located.

As suspected, Olivia was still at her desk, even though it was far past time for the doors to close. The black-haired woman, who was only two years older than Christina's thirty-three years, looked up in surprise, then smiled with pleasure when she spotted Christina standing in the open doorway of her office.

"Chrissy! You're back!" Jumping to her feet, she rushed around the wide desk and hurried over to give Christina a hug.

Unexpected tears burned the back of Christina's eyes as she held her friend tightly. "How are you, Ollie?"

"The same as usual. Going crazy with a stack of work in front of me and not enough time to do it all in."

Slipping an arm around the back of Christina's waist Olivia urged her over to a long leather couch positioned in front of a plate-glass wall overlooking the River Walk. This building was located in a beautiful area of town. Part of the office was furnished to the hilt with expensive antiques from the estate of Olivia's parents, who'd passed away ten years before in a plane crash. Losing her parents wasn't the only misfortune Olivia had faced. Olivia had become a partner of the reputable firm at an absurdly early age, but not without a price. She'd lost a husband along the way. But whether that was from Olivia's long hours at work or his roaming eye for the women would be hard to say. Their shared problems with love was just one of the many things Christina and Olivia had in common.

"Sit down, honey," she said to Christina. "Want some coffee? I'll call Mimi and have her make us a pot."

Christina rolled her eyes. "You mean you're making your poor assistant stay after hours? Really, Ollie, when are you going to slack up on this pace?"

Olivia's arms lifted, then fell uselessly to her sides. "I can't ever find a stopping place. But Mimi is being paid well, and she doesn't mind the extra hours, thank God. I really don't know what I'd do without the woman. It's a good thing she decided to come out of retirement." She sat down next to Christina and affectionately patted her knee. "Now tell me what you're doing here in the city. I thought you were making hay down on the farm."

"It's a ranch, Ollie. Remember? Just one of the biggest in the state of Texas. And I've been working on a case, not making hay."

Olivia laughed. "That's too bad. The way you described Mrs. Saddler's son, I thought things might be—" She broke off as she saw a pained look skitter across Christina's face. "Oh, don't tell me that I've actually hit a nerve."

Sighing, Christina said, "I don't want to talk about Lex Saddler right now. I came by to take a short breather before I make the trip back to the Sandbur. I've finished interviewing two of the three men that were with Paul Saddler the day he drowned."

Olivia's expression turned serious. "Oh. Did you glean anything from them?"

Wearily, Christina leaned her head against the back of the couch. She didn't know why she was so exhausted. Normally, she thrived on this part of investigating, but for some reason, leaving Lex and the Sandbur behind had been even harder this last time.

"I believe the men I spoke to are telling the truth about what they saw that day of the accident."

"So you couldn't trip them up—get them to change their testimony?"

"No. Oh, they both wavered a little from the initial facts they'd given twelve years ago. But I'm mainly going on their behavior as a whole. They both seemed genuinely sorry that Paul was gone."

"Hmm. Well, you ought to know. You've always had a canny knack for reading people."

Christina grimaced. She hadn't read Mike's true colors. And she wasn't sure she was seeing the real side of Lex, either.

"What about the third one?" Olivia asked.

"Lawrence Carter," Christina said. "Unfortunately, he's still out of town on business. And he's actually the one I wanted to talk to the most. So the meeting with him is on hold for right now."

Olivia's eyes narrowed. "Does he have a wife?"

Christina nodded. "He's got one now, but the one he was married to at the time of Paul's death divorced him not long afterwards. Whether there was some sort of connection there, it's impossible to say. I'd like to talk to that particular woman, but from what I can gather, she's moved to California. Anyway, he's currently married to a loud woman, who's beginning to get suspicious about me coming around asking to see her husband."

Olivia suggested, "Perhaps you should fly out to California and find the first wife. I'm betting she could tell you plenty."

Squaring around to face her friend, Christina sighed. "I still have a bit of work to do on Paul's things before I take that step. Besides, the only thing Lawrence Carter might be guilty of is taking a fishing trip with his friends."

Olivia nodded, then reached over and briefly squeezed her hand. "I've never seen you looking this tired, Chrissy. Haven't you been feeling well?"

"I'm fine. It's been—hectic this past week, and the weather has been so darn hot. What about you? Has the Miers case gone to trial yet? I know you've been worried about it."

Olivia said, "It starts tomorrow morning. That's why I'm here and probably will be here until twelve or one tonight. I'm not ready by any means. I can't find one witness to corroborate my client's alibi. Hell, I can't even find one person willing to be a character witness. On the outside, he appears to be a scumbag, but on the inside, I think he's just a scared little boy that got caught up in the wrong crowd. But that's another story." She smiled brightly as she ran her gaze up and down Christina. "Tell me where you found that sexy dress. I love it!"

Christina glanced down at the blue dress that Lex had given her. The garment was special to her, and she intended to enjoy it, even if she didn't know if their relationship would end as soon as Paul Saddler's case was finalized.

"Oh, I—picked it up down in Corpus this past week," she said as casually as she could.

Olivia continued to study her as though she were on the witness stand. "So you've been to Corpus, too. You're a lady on the move."

Christina shrugged. "Unfortunately, this case covers a lot of area."

"Well, I'm sure Mrs. Saddler is taking care of all your expenses. How do you like her?"

Christina's smile was genuine. "I like her very much. She makes no bones about speaking her mind, and that suits me. But I hardly ever see the woman."

"And her son?"

Groaning loudly, Christina rolled her eyes toward the ceiling. "I told you that I didn't want to talk about him."

"That's exactly why I do want to talk about him."

"Why do you have to be such a—lawyer?" Christina countered. "You think you have to cross-examine everyone that gets near you."

A wan smile touched Olivia's pretty face. "Only the ones I care about."

Olivia did care, Christina realized. She was one of the few people who would always be there for her through thick and thin, no matter what.

Restless now, Christina left the couch and walked over to the plate glass. The scene below was beautiful, with the narrow river lined with tropical trees and plants. Currently, people were gathered around park benches, cooling themselves in the shade. This city had always been her home, and she loved it, yet she was already yearning to head south to the Sandbur. To Lex. How could she have changed so much in such a short time?

"Okay, I'll just come straight out and tell you that I—I think I've fallen in love with the man."

Olivia's loud gasp had Christina turning to face the other woman.

"In love!" Olivia sputtered. "Are you serious? I was just hoping you'd been having a little fun with the man. And you hit me with something like this!"

Christina groaned again. "I realize it sounds crazy—"

"No, not crazy. Just unexpected," Olivia interrupted. "I mean, since you left Mike, you've been so determined to remain single and independent."

A chilly hand touched her heart, and she quickly looked back toward the river so that her friend couldn't see the pain on her face. "I figure I'm still going to remain single and independent."

"Why?"

She swallowed. "I don't think Lex Saddler is the marrying sort. And I'm stupid to let myself feel anything for him in the first place."

"Oh, honey, we don't *let* ourselves feel anything. That just happens whether we want it to or not."

Frustrated tears burned the back of her eyes as she looked over her shoulder at Olivia. "If that's true, then why do I have to feel things for the wrong kind of man? You would've thought Mike had taught me a lesson," she said, with a great deal of self-directed sarcasm.

Leaving the couch, Olivia walked up behind her. "Let's forget about your past for a minute. What about Lex? Why are you so sure he's not the marrying kind? Has he already been burned by one marriage?"

Christina shook her head. "No. As far as I know, he's never so much as had a fiancée. Just a string of girlfriends a mile long." Shoving a hand through her tousled red hair, she looked at Olivia. "He cares very much for his family and the ranch, but he says he's never been in love, and frankly, I don't think he ever will be."

Olivia frowned. "Honey, you could be wrong about him. I can't see you falling for a man that is incapable of loving."

"Oh, he's capable. He loves his family dearly."

"Family is different. That sort of love is something that starts as a baby and grows as you grow. Loving a spouse is an emotional tie—an investment that some men have trouble making. But you've not known this man for that long, Chrissy. He might decide he doesn't want to live without you."

Pinching the bridge of her nose, Christina sighed. "I don't know what to do. Lex says he cares about me, but he says that love isn't for him. And I'm scared. Scared that I'm getting myself into another hopeless situation. I groveled at Mike's feet for four long years. I did everything to make him see how much I cared—how much I wanted the two of us to be a real family—but in the end he didn't care one whit. I'm not about to humiliate myself like that again. Not for any man."

Olivia's fingers squeezed her shoulder. "Maybe this Lex Saddler isn't just *any* man."

Chapter Nine

Throughout the long drive back to the Sandbur, Christina thought plenty about Olivia's words. Lex Saddler really wasn't just *any* man. From what she could see, he wasn't the sort who lied and manipulated. He was decent and honest and hardworking. So what was the matter with her? Why wasn't she breaking her neck to jump into his arms and enslave him with her feminine charms?

Because she didn't want him to love just her body. She wanted him to love *her*. Totally. Completely. She wanted a man who would give her children, remain at her side even after she was wrinkled and gray. If Lex couldn't be that man, then she'd have to move on and forget him.

In spite of her miserable thoughts, though, her heart began to sing the moment she parked near the ranch house and spotted Lex walking across the lawn to greet her.

"I see you kept your promise and made it back safely,"

he said with a smile, then lowered his head and placed a swift kiss on her cheek. "Do you have bags?"

"One. In the backseat."

He fetched the bag, and Christina walked beside him as they headed to the house.

"So how did things go?" he asked. "No trouble?"

"No trouble," she said while her hungry eyes kept creeping over to his profile. Tonight he was dressed in a pair of old jeans and a faded red T-shirt. The sight of his bare arms reminded her even more of his wiry strength and how it had felt to have those arms wrapped tightly around her.

"I'm glad," he said. "I've missed you."

By now they'd reached the back entrance to the house. The porch light hanging to the left of the door shed a faint pool of light on his grinning face.

God help her, but just looking at him left her breathless and longing to kiss him and never stop. "And I've missed you, too," she said softly, then inclined her head toward the door. "Let's go in, and I'll catch you up on what I've learned."

When they entered the kitchen, she spotted Cook sitting at the long pine table, sipping from a tall iced glass.

"Good to see you back, young lady," Cook greeted her, with a smile. "Want to join me and Lex with something to drink?"

"Give me a minute to freshen up, and I'll be right back," Christina told her.

Grabbing her bag from Lex, she raced upstairs to her bedroom. After a quick visit to the bathroom and a hasty brush of her windblown hair, she hurried back down to the kitchen.

Cook patted the bench space next to her. "Sit here, Christina. Lex will get you whatever you'd like."

Glancing around the room, Christina eased down next to Cook. "Is Geraldine out for the evening?"

"She'll be gone for the next few days," Lex said from a spot at the cabinet counter. "Nicci had to go to a medical convention in Houston, and she wanted Mother to accompany her. They hardly get to spend any time together, so Mother agreed to go."

"I think that's very nice," Christina said, while wishing she could have had such a caring, responsible mother. As it was, Retha contacted her daughter in unpredictable spurts. There were times she'd go out of the country for weeks without letting Christina know of her whereabouts. But Lex's family was different. They were knit together with love. Oh God, why did she have to keep thinking of that word, *that* emotion?

Lex held up a coffee mug. "Would you like coffee or lemonade or soda?" he asked, then added, with a sly grin, "Whatever my lady desires."

My lady. Just hearing him say the words, even teasingly, made her heart beat faster. "Coffee would be great."

While Lex poured the coffee and added cream, Cook said, "We've been wondering if you got Paul's old buddies to tell you anything helpful."

Before she could make a reply, Lex arrived at the table with the coffee and took a seat next to Christina. His closeness was both sweet and tempting, making it difficult to focus on Cook's comment.

"I should have called," Christina said. "But since I didn't have anything concrete to report, I didn't want to get your hopes up."

Besides that, she didn't want Lex to think she couldn't go for two days without hearing his voice. She already felt as though she were wearing her feelings for him on her sleeve. Especially after giving him that melting kiss right before she'd left.

"Did you get to interview the men?" Lex asked.

"Two of them," Christina answered. "After Red's very young wife told me where to find him, I caught up to him on the golf course. I'm not sure he appreciated me showing up and interrupting his game. But he was polite enough. And I found Harve at his downtown office and didn't have any problem getting in to see him."

"What did you think about them?"

Shrugging, Christina took a careful sip from the steaming mug. "I'm not certain, but my hunch tells me that Red and Harve did nothing to harm your father."

Lex looked utterly surprised by her announcement. "Why would you think that?" he asked, with dismay. "Both Red and Harve lost almost everything they had in divorce battles. They both needed money and more than likely committed insider trading."

Christina shook her head. "That doesn't make them killers. And remember—I said this is just my hunch," she reminded him. "I've got to find proof before I can come to any sort of conclusion about this case."

"Forget about the stock thing," Lex countered. "There's the pertinent fact that the men could have taken Dad to Mustang Island or even Aransas Pass for medical help. Instead, they wasted precious time taking him back to Corpus! They waited about calling the Coast Guard! Shall I go on?"

"I'm aware of all of that, Lex. And, yes, it does look suspicious. But when people are in shock, they don't always do the right thing. It's my job to keep an open mind to anything and everything. And I'm not ruling Harve and Red out yet. Are they thieves? It smells like they are. Murderers? I'm not sure."

"Wait a minute," Cook interjected. "You haven't mentioned anything about that dried-up, scrawny Lawrence. What about him?"

Sighing, Christina said, "The maid said he still hadn't returned from his business trip. But I'm pretty sure he's having the house help lie for him. I think he is home and is doing everything he can to avoid talking with me."

"The little bastard," Cook muttered.

Lex clucked his tongue in an admonishing way at the older woman, and Christina could hardly keep from smiling at the two. If Lex could only love her a fraction as much as he loved Hattie, then she'd be a cherished woman for the rest of her life.

Cook scowled at him. "Well," she reasoned, "he was a cold little man, but Paul went out of his way to include him in parties and outings. I never could cozy up to him myself. He'd come back here to the kitchen, wanting a certain type of cup or glass. Or he'd want hot tea when everyone else was drinking iced—as though he was special or something. I remember Paul saying the man was a hypochondriac. Ran to the doctor for every little ache. I think he felt sorry for him."

"So you're thinking Lawrence is hiding from you because he might know more than what he told the police?" Lex asked Christina.

"We'll see. I've got someone staking out his house. If he's seen, I'll know about it. And when he does show his face he'll have to answer a few questions," she told him.

Lex was about to ask her another question when his cell phone rang. He answered it immediately, uttered a few short words, then snapped it shut. As he rose to his feet, he said, "I'm sorry, Christina. That was Matt. A buyer that was supposed to be here this morning has arrived tonight. He's over at the Sanchez guesthouse, and I've got to go welcome him. I'll be back as soon as I can."

Christina nodded that she understood. "I have plenty of work to keep me busy."

He tossed her an apologetic smile, then strode quickly out of the room.

As Christina watched him disappear, Cook said, "Lex has been worried about you."

Surprised, Christina turned her gaze on the older woman. "Did he tell you that?"

"Not in those exact words. But I could tell."

The idea that Lex had expressed any sort of concern about her to Cook plucked at Christina's heartstrings. "Lex cares about people."

Cook grunted with amusement. "Some more than others."

Afraid to analyze what Cook meant by that, Christina sipped her coffee and let a few moments slip by before she said, "Cook, you probably know Lex better than anyone here outside of his family. Why do you think he's never married?"

Cook's dark eyes softened as she looked at Christina. "That's hard to say. When he was younger, he used to tell me that he never knew if the girls liked him just for him or for his money. It ain't no secret that many a woman in these parts would have liked to set up camp here in the Saddler house. Can't blame any of 'em for trying, though. A wife of his wouldn't have to want for anything."

"No. I expect not," Christina thoughtfully agreed. She'd had her own problems with guys viewing her as a money machine. But she'd learned to spot the users, and no doubt Lex had, too. "But Lex is a smart guy. At his age, I'm sure he can spot a woman like that a mile away."

"Sure he can. That ain't the reason now."

"What is?" Christina persisted.

"I ain't sure. I expect his daddy dyin' had something to do with it. After Paul left us, Lex wasn't the same. Oh, don't get me wrong. He still liked the ladies, and they all seemed to fall in love with him, but he never looked at them in a serious way. Instead, he threw himself into runnin' the ranch. That's all that seemed to matter to him." A wan smile touched her red lips as she reached over and patted the top of Christina's hand. "A farmer has to invest a lot of time and work into makin' a crop grow. It's the same way with love. Lex just never took the time to plant the seed."

And if he planted the seed with her, would it grow? Christina wondered. Or would it wither and die, the way her parents' love had died?

Sighing, Christina rose from the table and carried her coffee cup over to the sink. "Thank you for the coffee, Cook. And the conversation. Now I'd better get to work."

"Work! Tonight? You just got here."

Nodding, Christina started out of the room. "I feel as though I'm getting closer to finding some sort of clue to pull this case together. I've got to keep searching."

She was about to push through the doors, when Cook said, "Christina, I guess you know that Lex is like a son to me."

Pausing, she looked back at the table, where Cook was still sitting. "Yes. That's always been obvious to me."

"I want him to be happy," she said. "And I believe you could make him happy, if you were so minded to."

Cook's words were so unexpected, so touching, that Christina's eyes stung with tears and her voice turned husky. "Thank you for saying that, Hattie."

Cook winked. "Don't thank me. Just remember what I said."

* * *

Almost two hours later, Christina was sitting on the floor in her makeshift office, sifting through the last of the manila files, when Lex knocked lightly on the open door.

"I saw the light from the hallway and figured you were still working. Don't you think you should put that stuff away and rest? All of this will still be waiting here for you tomorrow," he reasoned.

Instead of agreeing to quit for the night, Christina held up a sheet of paper and motioned for him to join her. "Come here. I want to show you something."

He grinned. "Forget the paper. I'm still waiting on my hello kiss."

"You'll have to wait a little longer. I think I've found something."

Curious now, he walked over to where she sat and peered over her shoulder at the paper she was holding.

"What is this?" he asked.

"That's what I'm trying to figure out. Your father scribbled some sort of list on this company stationery. Do you recognize the woman's name listed at the top?"

"Edie Milton," Lex voiced out loud. "Hmm. That sounds familiar."

"Apparently, your father had some sort of connection to this woman," Christina said.

He snapped his fingers. "I remember. She was secretary to Coastal Oil's CEO at the time Dad worked there."

She looked at him hopefully. "What about now? Is she still there?"

"No. About a year after Dad died, she was killed in a car accident. Her brakes failed, and she crashed into the back of a semitruck."

Christina's interest was piqued even more. "Do you have any idea why Paul would have put her name on a list?"

Shaking his head, Lex began to read the list out loud. "Edie Milton, Red's office, Lawrence's broker, Harve's wife, bank statements, photocopies, tape recorder with a question mark. I wonder what this means at the bottom of the page? See disk."

Christina glanced over her shoulder, and as her eyes met his, she could see that only a part of his mind was focused on the paper in her hand. The hungry, smoldering lights that flickered in the brown depths fed her need to be closer, to feel the warmth and the comfort of his arms around her.

Clearing her throat, she said, "That's what I was about to ask you. If he meant a computer disk, I've not found any of them in these boxes. Is this absolutely all your father's things?"

His thumb and forefinger cradled his chin as he glanced at the mounds of papers and other articles that Christina had already sifted through. "Well, Mom gave Dad a desk and computer for a wedding anniversary gift one year. After he died, I guess the sentimental attachment made it difficult for her to keep using them. But she didn't want to get rid of them, either, so she had us store the desk away in the attic and the computer in a downstairs closet. She'd planned one day to go through the computer, just to see if there were any photos or things on there that the family might want. But that day has never come. Nicci mentioned the computer to her not long ago, and she promised to check it out. But you see how it is with Mom. Her plate is always full."

"Yes, I do see. But I wonder why Geraldine didn't mention those things to me," Christina mused aloud.

Lex shrugged. "She probably figured the stuff was

personal, family-type things instead of work matters. Or she might have forgotten. Either way, it doesn't matter. If you're game for a little dust and heat, we'll go up to the attic and see if we can find anything."

"That would be great. If your father put information on a disk regarding this list, it might shed some light on what was taking place at the company. Especially with the stocks."

He frowned. "You keep coming back to those damned stocks. Why?"

"Because oftentimes one crime leads to another."

"That's what I was trying to tell you in the kitchen. We only have a suspicion that Harve and Red are guilty of insider trading. But if they are, they could be guilty of murder, too."

"It's possible. Even though I'm not getting those sorts of vibes from them. We need more information to prove that anything criminal took place. Let's hope something will turn up in the attic."

His heavy sigh whispered past her ear, and then his hand wrapped around her arm and tugged her around to face him.

"I'll take you to the attic in a minute," he said lowly. "But before we go, I want to talk to you. Not about Dad's case. About us."

Her heart shifted into high gear as she forced her eyes to meet his. "Lex, I'm not sure this is the right time."

"Why? You're not ready to hear that I've been thinking of you night and day?"

The soft huskiness of his voice sprinkled goose bumps across her skin. "Every woman likes to be remembered," she told him.

"And does every woman also like to be kissed?"

Her gaze landed on the hard curve of his lips, and suddenly her heart was pounding out of control as her body begged to get close to his.

"If the right man is doing the kissing," she murmured.

"Then maybe you'd better decide for yourself if I'm the right man," he whispered.

His head bent, and then his lips fastened over hers in a totally dominating kiss. In a matter of seconds, Christina was mindlessly winding her arms around his neck, fitting her body next to his. This connection to Lex was the very thing her heart was longing for, begging for, and she could resist him no more than a rose could resist the hot June sun.

In a matter of seconds, the kiss turned bold and hungry. Christina could feel her body heat skyrocketing, her lungs burning for breath. Sometime during the embrace, his arms had moved around her, crushing her against him in a way that plainly said how much he wanted her.

Her senses were about to dissolve into smoke when he finally tore his lips from hers and began to nuzzle the soft spot behind her ear.

"I've never had a woman get in my head the way you have, Christina. You've become an important part of my life. Does that mean anything to you?"

Torn by his question, Christina dropped her head and fought to keep her tears at bay. "Of course, it means something to me," she whispered. "But I—oh, Lex, I don't want us to start an argument about this tonight. I just got back here."

And she was too vulnerable and weary to resist him, she thought. If he continued to kiss her, she'd soon be willing to let herself believe that an affair with him was better than pining for a love she'd never have.

Sighing heavily, he curled his hand around her upper arm

and turned her toward the door. "All right. Let's go up to the attic and get this over with."

A few minutes later, in the upstairs hallway that led to several bedrooms, Lex pulled down a trapdoor and unfolded a built-in ladder.

"Better let me climb up first," he told her. "I know where the light switch is located."

"I'll be right behind you," she assured him.

Other than the kitchen, most of the ceilings in the ranch house were very tall. The height forced them to climb several rungs of the ladder. After Lex crawled inside the attic and switched on a light, he reached down and gave Christina a careful hand up.

"Whew! This place is stifling!" she exclaimed as she stood on her feet and looked around at the piles of furniture and stacks of cardboard boxes.

"There's an air conditioner in the window. I'll turn it on."

In a matter of seconds, cool air was blowing across the attic, though it would still be a while before it truly cooled the stuffy space. He walked back over to where Christina stood waiting. When he stopped in front of her, with only an inch or two separating their bodies, she could see his mind was still focused on her instead of on finding his father's things. And she didn't know whether to feel flattered or frightened.

"Is the heat up here doing something to your brain?" she asked. "We're not finding Paul's things like this."

"Downstairs, you wouldn't let me finish. And when I told you we'd come up here and get this over with, I didn't exactly mean finding Dad's things. I realize you don't want to talk about us. But I do."

His hands closed over her shoulders, and she groaned out loud. "Lex, for God's sake, now is not the time! I don't—"

He interrupted her words with a muttered curse. Then, sliding his hands to the back of her waist, he asked lowly, "What do you want from me, Christina? A declaration of love? Would that make you feel better?"

Anger sparked her blue eyes. "I don't want or need empty words, Lex. I've had those before."

His mouth tightened. "I'm not *him,* Christina. So don't try to make a comparison."

She swallowed, then cleared her throat. His touch, his nearness, was messing with her mind, mixing up every thought, every word she tried to form on her tongue. "I'm sorry, Lex. I'm not saying you're the same sort of man as Mike was." She drew in a painful breath, then slowly released it. "He was a liar, and you've been nothing but honest with me. You've not promised me rainbows and I'd much rather have that honesty from you than hollow platitudes."

As Lex's gaze swept over Christina's troubled face, he wondered why everything inside him was pushing and pulling, making him feel as though he were going to split apart. He cared about Christina. More than he ever thought he could care for any woman. But was it love? The only thing his heart was sure about was that he didn't want to lose her. He wanted their time together to go on and on. He wanted to be close to her and have her want to be close to him. If that was love, then he was a goner.

A heavy breath rushed past his lips. "If you don't want promises from me, then what do you want, Christina?"

Lex could see anguish swimming in the depths of her eyes, and then her lips parted as though she was about to speak. But long, tense moments passed before any words finally passed her lips.

"I don't know, Lex. I only know that I lost so much when I hung my hopes on Mike. When those hopes were crushed, my self-esteem crumbled along with them. So did my ability to trust—not just men, but everyone. I guess I need time. I need to see for myself that you're capable of having a serious relationship."

It infuriated Lex to hear her compare him to the sleaze that had dished out so many worthless promises to her. He'd seduced a few women in his time, but he'd never lied or led them to believe he was in love with them just to get them into his bed. And he wasn't about to start with Christina.

His hands splayed against her back as he inched closer to the front of her body. "I want you to assure me that you'll give us a chance, Christina. I'll court you. I'll show you—"

She interrupted his words by placing a gentle finger against his lips. "You're not the marrying kind, Lex. To even pretend that you are would only make you miserable, and that would make me miserable."

Wrapping his hand around hers, he pulled her finger away from his lips. "You couldn't know that. I don't even know myself whether I'm marriage material," he countered. Then, with a weary sigh, he moved away from her and stared, without seeing, at the stack of boxes in front of him. "You may not believe this, Christina, but by the time I became a teenager, I knew I eventually wanted to have a wife and family of my own. I wanted to be just like my father. He was always hugging and kissing my mother, making her laugh and making her happy. He was always there for us kids, guiding us, loving us and punishing us whenever we needed it. He and my mother together made an incredible team, and I wanted that very same thing for myself."

"That's what I meant, Lex, when I told you how blessed you were to have parents like yours."

Turning, he looked at her and, for a split second, felt his heart fall and crack, like a dove's egg spilling from its nest and hitting the ground. Pain splattered through his chest, the sort of pain he'd not felt since the moment he'd heard that he'd lost his father. His parents had been blessed to have shared so much love while they'd been together. The idea that he might be losing his chance at that kind of happiness with Christina pierced him deeply.

"I was blessed with great parents. But not with love," he said huskily.

Clearly perplexed, she walked over to where he stood. "What does that mean?"

Grimacing, he thrust a hand through his tousled hair. "My mother and father had a special love. And I wanted the same for myself."

"Wanted? You no longer want what they had?"

Groaning, he slid his hands up her back and curled his fingers over her shoulders. "It's not a matter of wanting, Christina. God knows I've tried to find love. Maybe that's the problem. Maybe I've tried too hard."

Her beautiful blue eyes were full of shadows as they studied his face.

"Are you trying to tell me that a man like you can't find anyone to love? That's ridiculous, Lex. You're a man with everything. Looks, wealth, intelligence. I'm sure women have been throwing themselves at you since your high school days."

"Oh, I've had more than one woman fall in love with me. And each time it happened, I tried like hell to love her back, to fall in love with her. But trying couldn't make it happen. I'd end up asking myself if I had the same deep feelings that my father had for my mother. Would I want her by my side for years to come? Would I give up my very life for her? The answers were always no. And then I'd feel even worse about the relationship and about myself. I'd wonder if I was completely heartless, and now—well, I'm not sure I know how to love. Or if I ever will feel that overwhelming emotion Dad felt for Mom."

Slowly, tentatively, her palms came to rest against the middle of his chest, and Lex wondered if she could feel his heart throbbing against her fingers. If she realized, even for one second, how much he wanted her.

"Lex, you can't *make* yourself feel something for another human being. Love comes to your heart on its own, without an invitation. Whether you want it or not. Maybe you ought to think about that."

Bending his head, he brushed his lips back and forth against her cheek. "I could think about it a lot better if you'd make love to me," he whispered huskily. "But I'm not going to push the issue with you anymore. A man has honor, too, you know. If we make love again, you're going to have to do the asking."

He released his hold on her shoulders and stepped back. Surprise flickered across her face.

"Do you really mean that?" she asked

"I'm not a wolf, Christina." Forcing a lightness he was hardly feeling into his demeanor, he gestured toward a narrow walking space between a pile of boxes and shrouded furniture. "And we've got work to do."

Lex turned to start down the walkway, only to have her grab him by the arm. Pausing, he looked at her expectantly, while secretly hoping and praying that she'd changed her mind about making love to him.

Clearing her throat, she said, "I just wanted to thank you, Lex. For sharing your feelings with me."

Sharing? No. He'd never been good at sharing his feelings. Not the deep ones, the ones that made him feel uncomfortable and vulnerable and even afraid. Was that what loving a woman was all about?

If it was, then Lex had just taken a mighty big fall.

Chapter Ten

Trying his best to push away the deflated feeling that had suddenly settled upon him, he said, "C'mon. It's getting late."

He nudged her shoulder, and the two of them began to wind their way through a maze of items, which had seemingly been forgotten. Layers of gray dust covered everything.

"It doesn't look as though anyone has been up here for a while," Christina commented.

"Mom sends the maid up here every now and then to get rid of some of the dust, but that doesn't happen very often," he told her. "They're always too busy with the regular household chores to deal with this."

At the far end of the attic, next to the outer wall of the house, Lex spotted his father's old work desk, which was covered with a pair of old tacked denim quilts.

"This was his desk," Lex told her as he removed the quilts

and tossed them to one side. "There's still stuff in the drawers. And a few things in the boxes beneath it."

"I'll go through the drawers in the desk while you pull out the boxes," Christina suggested.

"That's fine with me."

After a few moments, it was clear to Christina that there was a substantial number of notebooks and folders filled with all sorts of work projects pertaining to the Sandbur stored inside the desk drawers.

"This is going to take a while," she said. "Do you think we could carry all of this down to my office? It would be much more comfortable going through it there. I have to go through each paper to be sure I didn't miss anything."

"Sure. Let's put everything in boxes and carry them over to the ladder," he agreed.

It took several minutes to get all the boxes safely down the ladder and into her office. Before Lex set the last one down in the corner of the small room, Christina was already sitting cross-legged on the floor, rifling through the paper material. And from the intense look on her face, Lex knew she wasn't planning on breaking for the night anytime soon.

"I'll go make coffee," he told her.

Looking up, she gave him a grateful smile. "That would be great, Lex. But you don't have to stay up and help. This is my job, remember?"

He slanted her a wry glance. "I assured Mom that it was mine, too. And Paul was *my* father. I want to help."

During the next half hour, Christina and Lex dug for anything that could possibly be connected to the list she'd found earlier this evening. But so far they'd found nothing but Sandbur papers.

"Here's a receipt," Christina said as she ran her gaze over

the yellow square of paper. "For seventeen hundred dollars. Looks like it's from a jewelers in Victoria. In one corner Paul's written 'Keep hidden from Geraldine.'"

"What's the date?"

When she read the date, Lex chuckled. "That's two days before my parents' wedding anniversary. Dad probably bought her something in silver and turquoise. She loves the stuff, so he gave her a lot of it."

"Hmm," she said thoughtfully. "Everything I've discovered about Paul tells me he was a man who liked to make people happy."

Funny that she could see his father so clearly from just a piece of paper and yet she couldn't see how much Lex wanted, needed her. Or maybe she did see and had decided that wanting and needing just weren't enough to make her happy, he thought miserably.

"You're right. Everything he did, he did for others. He was a very unselfish man," Lex told her. "That's one of the reasons I never really suspected anyone of killing him. He was good to everyone. He didn't have any enemies."

"Yeah," she quietly agreed. "Just like I find it difficult to believe that Joel simply walked away from me—his only sibling."

The husky note in her voice had Lex glancing over to see her head was bent, and as he studied the crown of her shiny red head, he realized the mystery of her brother was still affecting her, the same way the puzzle of his father's death was now tearing at him. Christina had been right those few weeks ago when she'd first arrived on the Sandbur. Finding the truth was always important.

Forcing his attention back on the plastic container jammed between his knees, he continued to rifle through the contents, most of which seemed inconsequential. Until he reached the bottom, where he discovered a flat cardboard tin box.

"Here's a box with something rattling inside," he announced, with a bit of excitement.

Jumping to her feet, she hurriedly crossed the small room to where he was sitting. "Open it! It's probably the disk!"

Lex quickly opened the box, and Christina drew in a sharp gasp at the sight of several computer disks nestled inside the container. "Oh my! Let's pray that one of these disks will hold some clues, Lex!"

Lex began to sift through the disks. All of them had paper labels attached to the front, but most of them had either one or two words that meant little or nothing to Lex and Christina.

"Right," he said. "Let's see if we can find anything important on them."

She pulled out the desk chair and slipped into it. While she brought the computer to life, Lex shoved the plastic disk into the slot on the tower. The task forced him to bend close to her shoulder, and it was all he could do to keep from turning his head sideways and kissing her cheek, burying his nose in her fragrant hair. He'd told her he was no longer going to press her to go to bed with him. But he knew the bold promise was going to be hell to keep. Especially whenever he was near her like this.

Clearing his throat, he said, "These disks are nearly twelve years old. There's no telling what sort of program they were written on."

"True," Christina agreed. "But we might get lucky."

Fifteen minutes later, Christina didn't feel lucky at all. Instead, she wanted to throw up her hands and scream. None of the five disks they'd discovered in the box would open.

"The frustrating part of this is that we don't even know

if one of these disks is connected to the list your father made," she grumbled.

"That's true," Lex said from his perch on the corner of the desk. "That's why we've got to find a way to open and read them."

Christina sighed. "It shouldn't be this difficult to convert the text on a floppy disk," she said. "Do you have any more suggestions?"

He chuckled. "Me? Are you kidding? I keep track of my cattle sales on the computer, but that's the extent of my ability. What we need is a computer whiz."

A thoughtful frown crossed Christina's face. "I know a good one, but he moved away from San Antonio, and I have no idea how to contact him," she said glumly, then turned a hopeful look on him. "Do you know anyone? Some of your family?"

He searched his brain for a moment. "Mercedes. She's a whiz with computers."

"She's also pregnant," Christina added, "and suffering from horrible bouts of nausea and fatigue. It's already so late in the evening. She's probably in bed. Let's not bother her. Anyone else?"

Lex raked a hand through his hair as he tried to think. "Lucita. She uses them at school and at home." He glanced at his watch. "It's getting a little late, but she won't mind if I call her. She and Ripp are probably up with their new baby girl, anyway."

Pulling a cell phone from his shirt pocket, he searched until he found his cousin's number, then punched it in. After a couple of rings, Lucita answered it herself, and Lex quickly explained the problem to her.

"Do you have any suggestions for us?" he asked.

"The easiest way to make sure you can open the thing

without destroying the contents is to use the same computer it was created on. Do you still happen to have Uncle Paul's old computer stored away somewhere?"

Lex glanced at Christina, who was watching him expectantly. "Yes. Mom put it away in a closet. Thanks for the suggestion, Lucita. And before I hang up, how's little Elizabeth?"

Lucita's soft chuckle was full of loving pride. It made Lex feel good to hear his cousin's happiness. She'd been through so much tragedy, it was time her life had changed for the better.

"Right now Ripp has rocked his daughter and himself to sleep. So all is quiet."

"You'd better get off the phone and enjoy it," Lex told his cousin. "I'll let you know tomorrow how we got along with the disks."

The two cousins quickly exchanged goodbyes, and as Lex slipped the phone back into his pocket, Christina asked, "How is Elizabeth?"

Surprised that her first question would be about the baby rather than a solution to the disk, Lex said, "She's fine."

A wistful smile touched her lips. "I'd very much like to see her and Nicci's daughter before I leave the ranch. Geraldine tells me they're both perfect little beauties."

"Humph. She looks like Ripp. And I don't see him as a beauty. But I guess Mom knows about babies and how they'll look when they grow to a more human size. I sure don't." He eased up from the desk and walked over to a window where lights from the bunkhouse flickered through the branches of a live oak.

Behind him, he could hear Christina pushing back her chair, and he glanced over his shoulder in time to see her standing behind the desk, stretching her arms above her head. The sight of her curvy silhouette struck Lex with desire, and he was amazed at how much he wanted to take her upstairs to his bedroom, to take her into his arms and forget everything else.

"This probably sounds crazy coming from someone with a mother who is unorthodox, to say the least," she said quietly, "but I happen to think I'd make a good parent. I've already learned all the things *not* to do while raising a child."

The dim lighting of the room left soft lights and shadows flickering across her face. As Lex looked at her, he could easily picture her with a baby in her arms, cuddling, loving, nursing.

"That night of the roundup, when we talked a bit about children, you seemed eager to be mother. But you also seem like a career woman to me. Which one are you?"

Clearly unnerved by his question, she glanced down at the disks scattered across the desk. "I am a career woman. Because that's—that's all I have, for now."

The hollowness in her voice touched some place in him that was much too deep for comfort. He shoved his hands in his pockets and walked over to where she stood. "This Mike...did you want to have his children?"

Turning her back to him, she answered in a low, strained voice. "At one time. But I had no intentions of ever having a child out of wedlock." Sighing, she glanced over her shoulder at him. "If I'm ever lucky enough to have children, I want their lives to be totally different from mine. I want them to have two loving parents, who will always be around."

It was on the tip of Lex's tongue to tell her that he didn't want her having any man's child, unless it was his. Did that mean he wanted a deeper connection between them? One that would last forever? Did that mean he was falling in love with her? He'd never even imagined having children with any of the other women he'd dated.

The idea addled him, shook him right to the soles of his feet, and he was struggling to come up with some sort of reply to her comment when she thankfully changed the subject.

"What did Lucita suggest about opening the disks?"

He walked back over to where she stood. "I've got to fetch Dad's old computer from the closet. It should be compatible with the disks."

Ten minutes later, Lex carted the computer to Christina's office. Thankfully, it fired to life, and Christina didn't waste a moment thrusting one of the disks into the proper slot and punching in the cues.

They both held their breaths as the machine made a few ratcheting clicks, then continued to rattle and whir.

"This is taking forever," Lex complained after several moments passed without anything appearing on the screen. "Apparently, it's not working right."

"Be patient. This is an archaic machine. It takes time for it to work."

Nearly forty minutes later, after reading through three of the disks, they declared them totally unimportant and started on the fourth. By now, Lex was losing hope, but Christina was determined to keep searching.

"We have this disk and one more to examine," Christina told him. "If we don't find anything here, there may be more information in the rest of the things we brought from the attic."

Lex eased his hip off the edge of the desk and moved across the small room to the mound of things they'd carried down from the attic. "I suppose I could start looking for more while you read through that."

She tossed an apologetic glance at him. "It's getting late, Lex, and I know you have to be up early for work. You don't have to stay and help. Unless you want to."

He met her glance. "I want to," he said simply.

Christina's heart winced with emotion. No matter what happened in the future, it was sweet to have him working by her side, as though they were a real couple with mutual goals.

Sighing, she turned her attention back to the monitor and was immediately caught by the words that had just flickered onto it.

Leaning closer, she studied the typed information on the monitor. "Oh my," she breathed with hushed excitement, "Come here, Lex! I think we've found some sort of personal journal!"

Hurrying to the back of her chair, Lex hunkered down low enough to be able to read over her shoulder. After a few paragraphs, he felt himself going cold, and the words from the page rasped hoarsely against his lips as he spoke them aloud.

Tuesday. July 14th. I can't let my beloved Geraldine know what's going on. It would worry her sick. And if she did know, it might put her in danger. Her and our children. No, I must keep this to myself until I get more evidence.

Emotions suddenly strangled him and Christina continued on.

Wednesday. July 15th. Slipped into Lawrence's office while he was at lunch. Worse than I expected. He's getting info that only the president or CEO should know. Suspect the latter's secretary—Edie. Rumors she'll do anything for money. Met Lawrence in the hall. Not sure if he saw me come out of his office, but I believe he did.

Christina looked up to see that Lex was now leaning his hip against the edge of the desk. His fingers were kneading his closed eyes as though he was trying to rub away what he'd just seen.

The sight of his anguish tore Christina, but she realized he couldn't avoid the truth. No more than she could.

"Maybe I'd better read the rest of this to myself," she gently suggested.

"No," he said, his voice choked. "Go on. I want to know."

Forcing her attention back to the screen, Christina began to read aloud.

Thursday. July 16th. Pushed my luck and searched Red's office. Found nothing. Maybe the guy is more honest than I thought. He showed up before I could leave. I played it cool. Came up with the excuse that I was hunting for a lost folder on pipeline corrosion tests. He didn't appear suspicious, and I felt like a heel for spying on a friend.

When Christina ended the longer passage, Lex straightened to his full height and looked down at her. "Is that all he entered on that day?"

"That's all. Here's Friday."

July 17th. An hour before I left work, Lawrence stopped by my office and invited me on a fishing trip to Corpus tomorrow with him, Red and Harve. He threw this trip together quick. Why now? Harve was supposed to take his son to Dallas to visit relatives. And Lawrence didn't look me in the eye the whole time he was inviting me. Dear God, the little bastard knows I've figured out he's brewing up some sort of stock scheme. But whether Harve and Red know about his plot is unclear. I'm thinking about asking them point-blank. But what if they're in on it with him? What might they do? Insider trading is hard to prove without concrete evidence. I need time. But we're leaving the ranch at six in the morning.

With his fists gripped at his sides, Lex closed his eyes and groaned. "Christina, you can't imagine how it feels to hear the last thoughts that were going through my father's mind just before he was killed. It's almost as though he understood that he might be in danger, but he was more concerned about exposing a crime than he was about keeping himself safe."

"Obviously," Christina said sadly. "Here's the last entry. It was made early on Saturday, before he left the ranch.

Saturday. July 18th. Geraldine has suspected something is wrong for a couple of months now. She seems to think it's my health or, even more ridiculous, an affair with another woman. Oh God, I'm eventually going to have to tell her what this is all about in order to ease her fears. She's the only woman I will ever love.

Maybe it's a good thing she's away now, that she took our daughters on a summer trip to Europe. But I wish she was here. At least to warn her that this fishing trip might turn out to be dangerous. Lex and all the guys are over at Mission River on roundup. I need to let him know about this before I leave the ranch. But how?

The last time Lex had cried was the day they'd buried his father, but he was damned close to it now.

Christina's shocked gaze lifted up to his face. "Apparently, he didn't get a chance to send any sort of message to you."

He wiped a hand over his face. "Twelve years ago most people didn't carry cell phones around with them, especially when they were out in the middle of nowhere, working cattle. And if he left a note here at the house, no one found it."

"Oh, Lex, I—I'm so sorry. So sorry." Rising to her feet, she gathered his hands in hers and held them tightly.

He swallowed hard, then sucked in a long, bracing breath. "Somewhere in the deepest part of me, I feared that my father had been intentionally killed. But the idea was so horrible, so heinous, that I wouldn't allow the suspicion to bloom. I wanted to shove it all away, to pretend that I'd lost him simply because the Lord wanted to take him. But now—now I have to accept that it was nothing like that. He was murdered."

She nodded with grim certainty. "Circumstantially, this proves that there was a motive for his death and that it probably was plotted and planned ahead of time. But I'm afraid that none of this would prove the case in a court of law. Paul suspected that Lawrence knew he'd been snooping, but there's no hard evidence of insider trading, much less murder."

The misery in his eyes was suddenly swept away by outrage. "Lawrence—the wimpy little bastard—he was always scared of his own shadow. Apparently, he was afraid of my father, too. Afraid he would sic the law on him and expose his white-collar thievery." He jabbed his forefinger at the monitor screen. "Why wouldn't this journal work in a court of law? It was obviously written by my father!"

"But it doesn't offer proof, Lex, just theories. A good defense attorney would probably get it thrown out altogether.

No, we've got to think of some other way to prove this murder happened."

Lex inclined his head toward the boxes of papers they'd carried down from the attic. "We still have a few more things to go through. Maybe we'll find something concrete."

"Perhaps," she mumbled. Then, stepping past him, she began to pace thoughtfully around the room. "But I'm doubting we'll find the smoking gun we need. In his last entry, Paul spoke of needing more time. Clearly, he didn't have enough evidence to go to the police, so it's unlikely there would be anything here."

Frowning with frustration, Lex glanced her way. "Then what do you propose we do next?"

She paused in her pacing as a plan began to form in her head. "From what I can gather from the autopsy report, the coroner believed Paul had some sort of incident with his heart before he went overboard, but he indicated the cause of death was drowning."

"Where is this leading?"

"I've been thinking about this for a good while now, Lex. Your father had no outward injuries. No blows to the head, no suspicious bruises or cuts. I think Lawrence gave Paul some sort of drug that disabled him. Maybe he stabbed him with a syringe or put it in his beer. I don't know. But I believed he drugged him."

Lex stared at her, confusion furrowing his brow. "No! That couldn't be right. The drug would have shown up in the autopsy. Wouldn't it?"

"Yes, if it had been something very obvious. But some drugs slip under the radar, and a corpse has to have extensive testing for each individual drug before it can be detected. In Paul's case, that testing wasn't done. Probably for county expense reasons—particularly when there wasn't a reason to think that a murder had occurred."

"If you believe he was given some sort of drug," he said, "where does that leave us now?"

Christina walked back over to where he was standing. "On the offensive," she stated flatly.

"What does that mean?" he asked warily.

"It means that I plan to draw Lawrence out. Force him to expose his crime."

His eyes widened. "I—don't think I like the sound of this."

She held up her palms in an innocent gesture. "Look, Lex, I'm not going to do anything foolish."

"That's right. We're going to contact the police. Now. Tonight!"

"Forget that, Lex! I know what a police department does with mere suspicions—they put them on the back burner. Especially when a case was pronounced closed a long time ago. No, I've got to draw Lawrence out and then call the police in on this. Otherwise, they'll have no reason for an arrest."

He reached out and snared a desperate hold on her upper arm. Christina's head jerked up, and her gaze clashed with his.

"And just how do you plan to get Lawrence to incriminate himself? The man is obviously smart. Like a fox. Smart enough to hide his crimes all this time. If anyone would have asked me before, I would have told them that Red would've been the most capable of harming Dad out of the three. God, that shows you how wrong appearances can be! Lawrence used his mousy demeanor to mask all his guilty tracks!"

The touch of his hand on her arm was sending electric impulses straight to her heart, causing it to thump even faster. "I'm going to visit Lawrence and let him know that I've discovered how Paul really died. I'm going to step out on another limb and tell him that I know he gave Paul the drug that caused his death—that we have ironclad evidence against him."

"But we don't!" Lex countered.

"He won't know that I'm bluffing. I'm going to tell him that I'll take the evidence to the police—unless he agrees to pay Geraldine twelve million dollars. One million for each year that your father has been dead."

"Twelve million dollars! That's blackmail! What good is that going to do?" Shaking his head, he led her over to the desk chair and eased her down on the seat. "Have you gone crazy, Christina? None of this makes sense! We don't want money. We want the man arrested!"

She smiled patiently up at him. "That's right. I only want Lawrence to believe the blackmail scheme. He's not going to want to shell out the millions—he might not even have that sort of money now, anyway—so when he tries to make a deal, I'll be wired, with the police listening in."

Frowning, he framed his chin with a thumb and forefinger. "I don't like it. He might get wise, and then where would you be?"

"I'm a trained police officer, Lex, and I'll have the help of the San Antonio police to help me with the wiring. I can do this."

Groaning, he pulled her to her feet while his gaze desperately searched her face. "You won't be going to see Lawrence unless I go with you!"

Amazed by this protective attitude, Christina stared at him. "Absolutely not! Your presence would ruin everything. I want him to believe that Geraldine and I are the only ones who know about his crime. That she has the evidence locked away in a safe. He'll figure he can handle two vulnerable women. In the meantime, your mother is away for the next few days, so she won't be put into any sort of danger."

His eyes widened as though he couldn't believe her audacity. "But what about you? You're setting yourself up to be either harmed or killed! I won't allow it! I'll take this—" he jabbed a finger at his father's old computer "—to the police first!"

Christina frowned. "They didn't do a very good job on this case the first time. Are you willing to chance that happening again? To risk letting your father's killer remain free? I'm sure as hell not!"

He suddenly wrapped his hands over her shoulders, and Christina did her best not to shiver as his green eyes bored into hers.

"What I'm not willing to risk is your life, Christina!"

Something about his voice, the passionate blaze in his eyes made her almost believe that he cared about her, that he wasn't just trying to play macho man. But to let herself think in those terms would only be setting herself up for a far bigger hurt than anything Lawrence might try. Only a few hours ago, Lex had admitted that he'd never fallen in love before.

But there could be a first time, Christina.

Not about to let herself dwell on the tempting little voice in her head, she tried to reassure him. "I promise not to meet Lawrence in a secluded place with no one else present. Will that make you feel better?"

His jaw remained hard and unyielding, yet she could see the light in his eyes turning tender, and it was that gentleness that nearly had her breaking down and promising to let the authorities take over the investigation. But twelve years ago the authorities had missed their chance to find the truth. For Lex's sake, and for his late father, she had to bring it out in the open.

"Not really. I'd like to forbid you to get anywhere near Lawrence! But I'm smart enough to know those old-fashioned manly tactics won't work on you."

Her expression wry, she rose to her tiptoes and pressed a kiss on his cheek. "Thank you for understanding that much." With her feet back on the floor, she allowed her hand to slide up and down his forearm in a reassuring way. "This will all be over with soon, Lex. And your life will get back to normal."

Tonight the discovery of his father's journal had taken her a giant leap closer to finishing this case, Lex thought. And once that happened, she'd be leaving the Sandbur for good. How could his life be normal then? She'd changed his life. She'd changed him. So what was he going to do about it?

Chapter Eleven

"Hattie, I think this is the wrong thing to do!"

The next morning, long before daylight, the old cook stared in dismay at Lex as he angrily paced up and down the long kitchen.

"You need to remember that Christina is in charge of this investigation," she pointed out. "You ain't in no position to be telling her how to do her job. Think about it, son."

Lex skidded to a halt in front of Cook, who was standing at the kitchen counter, pouring a cup of coffee.

Grimacing, he jabbed the air with his forefinger. "Policemen have partners for a reason. No law officer in his right mind tries to handle a job alone. And that's just what she's doing."

Cook picked up a plate of bacon and eggs and carried it over to the kitchen table. "Quit preaching," Cook scolded.

Annoyed that the woman wasn't taking his side in things,

he stalked over to the table and threw a leg over the bench that served as seating. "I'm only trying to save her neck."

"Humph," Cook snorted sarcastically. "That's not the way I see it."

"Hattie, you know I love you, but you'd better hush, or I'm going to lock you in the pantry."

"You'd have a hell of a time doin' that, sonny," Cook warned as she headed back to the gas range. "I may be gettin' a little age on me, but I can still put up a good fight. What you need to do is leave Christina alone and let her do her job."

Leave her alone. Maybe that was his whole problem right there, Lex thought grimly. He didn't want to leave the woman alone. He couldn't. When he tried to imagine himself moving on to other women, other interests, all he could see was a blank hole. Last night, when she'd returned from her trip to San Antonio, something had happened to him. He couldn't explain it or understand it. He'd wanted to find her ready to fall into his arms. That hadn't happened. She'd seemed even more resolute about not making love to him. And then, when she'd talked about her parents and children, about all the things she'd missed and longed for, he'd felt scales peeling from his eyes. Suddenly, he was viewing all his past relationships in a new light, and all the things he'd thought he would never want or care about had taken on new significance.

"Hattie," he said quietly, "last night we showed you Dad's journal. You read it. You know what happened. Lawrence is a killer."

Returning to the table, the old woman patted his back. "Lex, your daddy died a hero, and Christina will soon make sure that everyone knows it. I love her for that. And so should you."

Love Christina? Is that what this anguish inside him was? Is that why he was frightened out of his mind to let her get near Lawrence? Is that why he couldn't bear to think of this ranch without her on it? If all of this meant he was in love, then love was making him more miserable than he'd ever been in his life.

An hour later, as gray light was straining to get through the limbs of the live oaks shading the front yard, Lex followed Christina onto the front porch. The only thing she was carrying was a small beige handbag. Inside it was a pocketbook with identification, credit cards and a small amount of cash. The handbag also held a single tube of lipstick, a compact, a cell phone and a loaded snub-nosed .38 revolver.

"When do you expect to be back?" he asked as she paused on the top step.

"This evening. Hopefully before dark. If I can find Lawrence at home, this little tête-à-tête shouldn't take long." She looked at him, and the stark longing on his face made her want to fling her arms around his neck, to assure him that she would return safely. But what good would that do? she asked herself. It would only send him mixed signals, and every time she touched the man she lost a little more of her heart. If she didn't wind this case up and leave the ranch soon, there would be little of her heart to drag back to San Antonio.

"Christina, last night—I'm sorry I questioned your plans to nab Lawrence. You're the professional. And I was letting my personal feelings get in the way of everything else."

Even though the early morning temperature was past seventy, she felt the urge to shiver. She'd never expected him to utter such words to her, especially right now, and it shook the ground beneath her.

Swallowing, she glanced across the lawn to where one of the yellow curs was stretched out beneath the shade of a live oak. The dog appeared to be dead tired from rounding up cattle the day before, but if Matt or Lex was to whistle at him, he'd be up in a flash and ready to go. In many ways, Christina felt just like the cur. A word, a touch, a look from Lex made her long to please him, to give him anything and everything. Yes, she loved him. But she was determined not to fall in the hopeless trap she'd found herself in with Mike. She wasn't going to live on half-baked promises.

Glancing back at him, she tried to keep all emotion from her face. "And just what are your feelings, Lex?"

He moved forward, and her heart quivered as his fingertips came to rest beneath her cheek. "I think we need to talk about that, Christina. Tonight, when you come home."

Come home. If only he knew how much those two words meant to her. If only he meant them in the true sense of the word, she thought longingly. Her heart would sing loud enough to be heard in heaven.

"Yes," she said lowly, "we'll talk." Before she'd left Olivia's office, the other woman had pressed Christina to tell Lex that she'd fallen in love with him. Maybe her friend was right. Maybe it was time to let him see exactly what he was doing to her, and then she could see for herself if he really cared.

Her eyes closed against the emotions bombarding her, and she felt his lips pressing first against her forehead and finally against her lips.

"Be very careful," he whispered.

The lump in her throat made it impossible to speak, so she simply nodded and hurried off the steps before he could see the tears welling in her eyes.

By mid-morning, after checking at Lawrence Carter's

office and being told the man wasn't there, Christina was pulling into the elaborate drive circling the front of his house. To most regular folks, the place would be considered a mansion. Even so, the estate wasn't nearly as elaborate or stately as Red's or Harve's, and she wondered if the nervous little guy had deliberately kept his lifestyle modest so as not to draw attention to himself.

The front entrance was flanked by two tall Norwegian firs. As Christina punched the doorbell, she turned her back to the double doors and peered carefully around her. The neighborhood was extremely quiet, without so much as a bark of a dog to interrupt the twitter of birds perched on an ornate birdbath adorning the front lawn. Lawrence Carter lived in a very upscale area of the city, she thought grimly, and all at the expense of Paul Saddler's life.

"Yes? May I help you?"

Christina turned toward the young maid. "I'm here to see Mr. Carter. And before you tell me he isn't home, I know better. So you go tell your boss that I have some interesting information for him."

With a startled look, the maid said, "Yes, ma'am. Just a moment, please."

Leaving Christina standing on the porch, the maid hurried away, and then less than a minute later, a soft voice sounded behind her.

"Good morning. You were asking for me?"

Christina turned to see Lawrence had partially opened the glass door to stand on the threshold. His sparse hair was a drab ash-brown and plastered carefully to one side of his head. He was dressed all in polyester, as though his wardrobe was still stuck in the eighties. The brown slacks and yellow printed shirt looked hot enough to roast a pig.

"Good morning, Mr. Carter. I'm Christina Logan. I've been hired by Geraldine Saddler to look into her late husband's death. I'd appreciate it if you could answer a few questions I have. I promise not to keep you long." She glanced at her wristwatch as though she were in a great hurry. "I have a meeting across town, so I can't dally, anyway."

Faint annoyance registered on his thin face. "I…really don't have time." He glanced nervously over his shoulder. "My wife and I are getting ready for a little vacation."

"Oooh," Christina drawled pleadingly. "Couldn't you give me just five minutes? Red and Harve have already been so helpful in this matter. I'm certain your memory will be even better than theirs." Plastering a smile on her face, she stepped closer. "You don't have to invite me in. If you prefer, we can talk right here."

Clearing his throat, he quickly shut the door behind him and hurried her off the concrete porch. "Uh—let's go around to the side of the house," he suggested. "I really don't want my wife to hear this."

"I'm sure," Christina said under her breath.

She followed Lawrence along a cobblestone path until they reached a grouping of wrought-iron furniture sitting in the shade of a Cyprus tree. She'd promised Lex not to meet the man in private, but here on the lawn could hardly be called that. Especially when the wife was most likely watching from a nearby window and would clearly burst out of the house if she saw her husband physically attacking a woman.

Christina casually took a seat on one of the chairs, but the older man didn't appear to be interested in sitting. Instead, he stood a few steps away from her, his arms folded protectively against his scrawny chest.

"I'll be honest, Ms. Logan. My wife told me you'd asked to

speak to me, and Harve already told me that you'd been around asking questions. Frankly, I don't get it. Everyone, even the police, knows that Paul's death was a terrible accident."

"Well, I'll be frank with you, Mr. Carter. Geraldine has never been satisfied with the police's theory. And some information has come to light that proves her suspicions right." She crossed her legs and smoothed her fingers down her calf. Lawrence Carter might be a nerd, but he was still a man, and she wanted him distracted. She wanted him to be totally off guard when she gave him the news. "And I thought you'd be interested in hearing it."

His eyes narrowed shrewdly, yet the sight of his Adam's apple bobbing up and down his skinny neck said she'd rattled his nerves.

"Information," he repeated slowly. "You mean—about Paul's death?"

"I'm not calling it a simple death, Mr. Carter. I'm calling it murder."

If she'd slapped the man on both sides of the face, she couldn't have shocked him more. The blood drained from his skin, leaving his face the color of a sick mushroom. His jaws flopped as though they'd suddenly become unhinged.

"Murder?" he finally echoed. A nervous titter rushed past his colorless lips. "You must be mistaken, Ms. Logan. Paul wasn't murdered. The autopsy proved that."

With a catlike smile, Christina shook her head. "No, the autopsy proved that Paul drowned. But I've discovered why he drowned and I have the evidence to prove it."

She'd say one thing for him: the skittish little man did a quick job of gathering his composure. He smiled faintly and pleated his hands in front of him, as though he had all the time in the world to discuss the matter.

"If you have all that, why come to me?"

She tapped the air with the toe of her high heel. "Well actually, I'm not here to get your recollection of that day Paul was killed. I already know how it all happened. Paul drowned because he was unable to swim and save himself. You made certain of that when you gave him succinylcholine to make his muscles useless. In that condition, it was easy to nudge him overboard while the other two men weren't looking. And with just enough of the muscle relaxant in Paul's system, he'd never be able to swim. Never be able to take the facts of your insider trading to the police."

The man's sharp features hardened. "You're bluffing. I didn't leave any—"

She didn't hide her loathing as she stared at him, waiting for him to hang himself. "Go on, Carter. You were about to say you didn't leave evidence? If you want to take the chance that I'm bluffing, then by all means go ahead. But Geraldine has it safely tucked away, just waiting to hand it over to the DA. Unless...you're interested in making a deal."

To her surprise, the man marched toward her, his eyes filled with a menacing light. She discreetly opened the latch on her handbag and prayed he would decide to play it cool with her.

"What sort of deal?" he asked gruffly.

The question was a complete admission of guilt, but Christina wasn't surprised by it. She was just thankful her plan was working.

"Geraldine actually wanted you to rot away in prison, but I convinced her that was too easy. A man like you values his money far more than his freedom. So she's decided she'll sell you the evidence for the neat little sum of twelve million. One million for each year she's had to live without her husband."

The scrawny man's eyes began to bulge, and Christina realized he was struggling to keep from gagging.

"That's blackmail! And there's nothing you could have on paper that could incriminate me!"

Christina enjoyed giving him a sickeningly sweet smile. "Who said anything about it being on paper?"

His narrow eyes cut across her face, and then his gaze turned to the house behind them. Whether he was thinking about the luxurious digs or the loud wife inside was impossible for Christina to guess.

"I don't have twelve million dollars," he muttered.

"You work for a bank. You can get it."

Spluttering, he jerked his gaze back to her. "That sort of money is difficult to get. It might take weeks, even months!"

"Geraldine doesn't have that long to wait. We're giving you two days."

Pure venom was etched upon the man's face. "The woman doesn't need money! I've never had a fraction of what she's got!"

Rising to her feet, Christina said, "It's not the money she wants. It's retribution. And this is her way of getting it." She pulled a card from her handbag and handed it to him. "Here's the time and place we'll make the exchange. Red Road Inn—it's just off I-10. Make sure you're there no later than three-thirty, or we're going straight to the police."

He read the information on the card, then jerked his attention back to her. "This is a busy truck stop! Are you crazy?"

"What sort of meeting place would you prefer? A quiet, dark alley? We're not the crazy ones here, Mr. Carter."

With that, she swished past him and began to walk toward the front of the house, where she'd left her car. Before she'd taken five steps, he caught up to her.

"Does anyone else know about this?" he asked in a hushed voice. "Has Geraldine told her family?"

Christina summoned all the acting ability she possessed. "Your questions are getting stupid—especially for a supposedly smart man like you. Do you think she'd want her family to know she's committing blackmail? No. Only she and I know, and that's the way things will stay. Once we turn the evidence over to you, that will be the end of this. You'll be out of Geraldine's hair, and we'll be out of yours. Deal?"

He hesitated, but only for a moment. "Yeah. It's a deal."

Later that night at the Sandbur, Cook served Christina and Lex a special dinner of shrimp jambalaya, along with an assortment of fresh seafood. The mini feast was meant to be a small celebration for uncovering the truth about Paul's death. But Lex hardly appeared to be in a celebratory mood.

Throughout the meal, he remained quiet and only picked at the food on his plate. God knew, he had plenty on his mind, Christina thought. He'd already expressed his concern over the plan she'd hatched to allow the police to catch Lawrence red-handed. But a part of her wondered if his sober demeanor might have something to do with the talk he'd requested that morning. He'd seemed so serious when he'd said they needed to talk. Was he going to tell her he'd lost interest?

He could have sex with most any woman he wanted. He doesn't need to wait around on you.

That little voice inside her head had pestered her throughout the drive back from San Antonio and was still gnawing at the back of her mind, making it impossible to think about little else.

Maybe she'd been wrong all along by putting a halt to

their physical relationship. Their night together in Corpus had rocked her, transported her to the closest thing she'd ever experienced to heaven on earth. But even more than that, she'd felt a connection to Lex that superseded anything she'd ever imagined. She didn't want to lose that. Lose him. Yet she didn't want to let herself slip into a relationship that might never go further than the bedroom.

The two of them had just finished dinner and were retiring to the living room when Lex's sister Mercedes stopped by to discuss the progress they'd made on Paul's case. While she and her brother talked, Christina excused herself, stepped out on the front porch, and made a phone call to Geraldine to let her in on the plans she'd made with the authorities in San Antonio to attempt to catch Lawrence. Geraldine was eager to have the man convicted and put behind bars, but she was also concerned about Christina's welfare.

She reassured Lex's mother as best she could and ended the call just as brother and sister emerged from the house.

The pretty blonde walked over to where Christina was sitting on a wicker love seat.

"I wanted to thank you," she said, "for what you've done for our family. It was very hard for me to hear that my father was murdered. Especially by that creepy Lawrence. But at least we know the truth now."

Christina smiled gently at Lex's sister. "It's not completely over yet, Mercedes. But I promise I'll do everything I can to help convict the man."

"I wish I could be more help," Mercedes said as her hand slid protectively to her belly, "but I've not exactly been feeling up to par here lately."

Rising from her seat, Christina gave the woman's shoulders an affectionate hug. "You shouldn't worry about that for one minute. The important thing is to take care of yourself and your baby. Besides," she added impishly, "Lex has made a great Dr. Watson."

Mercedes turned an affection grin on her brother. "Lex is a man of many talents—when he wants to be. You should get him to tell you about riding broncs on the college rodeo team. He was a wild man in those days."

"Mercedes!" he scolded lightly. "Christina doesn't want to hear about that."

Laughing now, the woman stepped off the porch. "I'm heading home. Gabe will be worried if I don't show up soon."

She waved goodbye, then climbed in a black pickup truck and drove away.

Once she was gone, Christina sank back onto the love seat. "I like your sister very much. I wish I could've gotten to know her under better circumstances," she said.

Lex strolled across the porch and took a seat beside her. When he reached for her hand, Christina felt the gentle touch all the way to her heart, forcing her to bend her head to hide the emotion on her face.

"I like my sister, too, but I've been counting the minutes until we could be alone," he said quietly. "I was so relieved when I saw you return to the house this afternoon. I kept having this awful vision of Lawrence trying to harm you."

She looked up at him, and it suddenly struck her that he had been well and truly frightened for her safety. The idea made her heart want to hope that he might actually care for her, that his caring might one day turn to love.

"Whenever I told Lawrence that your mother wanted money, I honestly believed he could have put his hands around my neck and choked the life out of me. But I knew he wouldn't. The man is the epitome of a wimp. Still, he's dangerous. I have no doubt about that."

His fingertips began to slide gently against the back of her hand. "I kept imagining him following you, maybe trying to run you off the highway. Sometime back, that happened to my cousin, Luci. And she could have easily been killed."

"Well, thankfully, neither he nor anyone else followed me. Now we've got to hope that Lawrence will be desperate enough to show up at that restaurant with a satchel full of money."

With a slight shake of his head, he tightened his fingers around her hand and leaned his face toward hers. "I don't want to talk about that anymore tonight, Christina. I want to talk about you—us. You said you wished that you'd met Mercedes under different circumstances. Well I can't help but wonder how things would've been if we'd met some other way."

"I'm not sure we would have met. I live in San Antonio. You live here. Our paths would have probably never crossed."

"No. You're wrong about that. We were meant to meet." His eyes softly roamed her face. "I've been thinking a lot, Christina, about that night we spent out on roundup. You seemed like you really enjoyed being outdoors with the cowboys and the horses—and me."

She looked away from him while wondering why her heart was hammering, why she suddenly felt so scared. Funny how she'd faced plenty of dangerous situations during her years as a law officer, yet none of them shook her like the thought of never having this man's love. In some strange way, the night they'd spent sleeping in bedrolls under the stars had affected her even more than the night they'd actually made love. Something about sharing that part of his life had given her an even deeper glimpse of the man than being physically connected to him had.

"I did really enjoy it," she told him, then tried to laugh to ease the turmoil in her heart. "I thought sleeping on the ground would kill me, but it didn't."

His fingers continued to massage the back of her hand. "Not very many women like the ranch. Not after they're on it for any length of time," he admitted. "It's very isolated."

"I don't think of it as being isolated. The ranch is always full of activity—a little settlement unto itself."

His eyes grew warm and tender, but then he quickly looked away, as though he was embarrassed that he'd let his emotions show. "You're different, Christina. From the moment I met you, I realized that, but I didn't want to admit it to myself."

His gaze turned back to her, and this time there was a hint of regret on his face. "I've been looking at everything—at you—in the wrong way."

Christina couldn't stop her groan. "Oh please, Lex, don't expect me to believe that you've had this sudden emotional lightning bolt hit you and you think it's love. I—"

"I wasn't going to tell you that I love you. I wouldn't do that unless I was sure. I'd never lie to you like that. Besides, you wouldn't believe me if I said such a thing to you."

Feeling as if she was being torn to shreds, Christina rose to her feet and walked to the edge of the porch. With her back to him, she said, "I'm glad you realize that."

Long, pregnant moments passed before he moved behind her and slipped his arms around her waist. "I guess I want you to understand how important you've become to me."

Christina was suddenly trembling all over, as though she was standing on a dangerous precipice and the slightest breeze might topple her over. Everything inside of her was urging her to turn to him, to tell him that she loved him. Loved him utterly and completely.

I've had more than one woman fall in love with me.

The words Lex had spoken to her in the attic were suddenly spinning through her head, blocking the vow of love from spilling from her lips. He'd been told by more than one woman before that he was loved, but that obviously hadn't brought out any sort of commitment from him. And like he'd said, it certainly hadn't made him love the women in return. It would be stupid of her to think that telling him she loved him would somehow fix anything.

Bending her head, she pushed the next words past the lump in her throat. "I believe that, Lex."

Instantly, he turned her toward him and fastened his lips over hers. As soon as the soft, moist curves yielded beneath his own mouth, hunger struck him hard while, at the same time, joyous bells clanged in his head. She was the very thing his heart, his soul, had been searching for. He didn't just want this woman; he *needed* her.

Once the kiss threatened to completely steal his breath, he broke the contact between their lips and mouthed against her neck, "You can believe me, darling."

Suddenly her hands were in the middle of his chest, levering a small, cold gap between them. The forced separation had him looking questioningly down at her.

Her beautiful features were full of pain, and the sight totally confused Lex. The only time he'd ever made women miserable was when he'd given them a final goodbye. Yet Christina seemed to be just the opposite. The closer he tried to get, the more miserable she appeared to be.

And it suddenly struck him that making love to Christina, hearing her say their relationship would keep going, was only a tiny portion of what he wanted. He wanted her to be happy, deep-down happy. He wanted to love her. Really love her.

Oh God, what was happening to him? he wondered. And what could he do about it now? She'd never believe he was falling in love with her. He wasn't even sure he could believe it himself.

"I—um, I'm sure you're very tired," he said gently. "And I've got a long day ahead of me tomorrow. Maybe we'd better say good night."

The relief on her face actually stung him, but then she gave him a wobbly smile, and his heart felt like a piece of iron that had just been thrown into a smelting pot.

"I think you're right," she said, then carefully eased out of his arms. "I've got a busy day tomorrow, too, getting things coordinated with the Bexar County Sheriff's Department."

To his surprise, her eyes suddenly turned watery, and for one split second, he started to jerk her back into his arms, to beg her to listen to what had just dawned in his heart. But she needed time, he realized. And he did, too. Time to figure out how to prove his sincerity, his newfound devotion to her.

When you love a person the way I loved your father, you just know.

A few days ago, Lex couldn't comprehend what his mother had once told him about falling in love. But now the meaning of her words was crystal clear to him. He loved Christina, and because he did, he saw more, felt more, understood things that had only been mysteries to him before. It was like stepping into a new world, and even though the path was scary, he realized he had to keep walking ahead.

With a wry smile, he stepped forward and ran a gentle hand over her red hair. "Don't worry, my sweet. Everything is going to be all right."

Chapter Twelve

The next day, in spite of spending most of her time on the telephone with one law official after another, Christina couldn't shake Lex's parting words of the night before.

Everything is going to be all right.

What had he meant by that? Had he been talking about the sting to catch Lawrence or their fragile relationship? God, she wished she'd questioned him before he'd left the porch and retired to his room.

She'd thought she'd have a chance to speak with him this morning, before the day became hectic, but her sleep had been erratic, and by the time she'd finally pushed herself out of bed and stumbled down to the kitchen for breakfast, Lex had already left the house.

Now it was growing late in the evening, and he was quite late in returning to the house. Cook had prepared supper, but Christina had told the woman to put the whole meal in the warming drawer. Sharing supper with Lex had become her favorite part of the day, and she wanted to enjoy it for the few evenings that were left before her time here on the ranch was over.

She was in the den, going over a folder of information she planned to hand over to the DA while watching the evening news on the television, when she heard a vehicle drive up at the west end of the house.

Since Lex always parked his truck in that area and entered the house through the kitchen, she jumped from the couch and hurried through the house to greet him. Just knowing he was home filled her with relief. For some unexplainable reason, she'd been anxious about his safety.

By the time she reached the kitchen, she expected to find Lex already there. But the room was empty, and an odd feeling of alarm sent a chill through her.

Something wasn't right.

She stepped onto the back patio and glanced toward the west end of the house. When she did, her breath caught in her throat as a sinking feeling hit the pit of her stomach.

Lawrence Carter was walking rapidly toward her. And from the cold look on his face, he wasn't on the ranch to make a deal. Why hadn't she guessed something like this could happen?

Of all the days for Lex to be delayed, this wasn't the one he would have chosen. He'd planned on being home early this evening to eat supper with Christina, and then he'd planned on taking her on a leisurely drive over a few parts of the ranch she'd not yet seen. She'd been working herself to the point of exhaustion over his father's case, and he wanted her to relax, to forget about Lawrence Carter and insider trading and paralyzing drugs. But mostly he simply wanted to be alone with her, with no outside distractions.

But one problem after another had occurred today, and he'd spent the past four hours helping the hands move a herd of cows from a pasture with a broken windmill to an area of the ranch where water was plentiful.

After unsaddling Leo and leaving him in the capable hands of a stable groom, Lex left the horse barn and started across the ranch yard on foot. Since most of the cowboys had already retired to the bunkhouse, the work area was quiet, and the long shadows of evening were beginning to cool the hard, packed earth.

Halfway to the house and lost in thought, he was faintly surprised when he suddenly spotted his teenage niece, Gracia, riding one of her cutting horses toward him. Normally, she rode those particular horses only in the practice arena.

When she reached him, she pulled her mount to a rapid stop. "You're out late this evening," she observed.

"So are you, young lady. Why aren't you riding in the arena?"

She shrugged. "Cloud Walker needed a bit more exercise, so I rode him down the road for a couple of miles." She wrinkled her nose and glanced back in the direction she'd just traveled. "Who is that creepy man at Aunt Geraldine's house? I saw him on the back lawn with Christina. They were walking together toward the house. Christina was smiling like he was a friend, or it looked like she was smiling. Is he a guest of hers?"

Icy fear rushed through Lex as his gaze shot past Gracia and on toward the house. "A man? What did he look like?"

She made a face of disgust. "Like a weirdo. Skinny and sorta old, with plastered hair. What is he doing here?"

Jerking his cell phone from the pocket of his jeans, he tossed it to the teenager, then took off in a run toward the house. "Call your father, and tell him what's going on!" he shouted over his shoulder. "Now!"

As Christina reentered the house, her mind was frantically searching for a way to deal with the maniac pointing an automatic pistol at her back.

Clearly, he had evil on his mind, and she had to think fast to come up with some diversionary tactic and snatch the weapon from him before he decided to use it.

As they walked into the kitchen, he asked gruffly, "Who else is in the house?"

"I don't know," she lied. "The maids could be upstairs."

Christina wasn't about to tell him that Cook and the maids had left hours ago. With Lex still out working, there was no one here but her.

"What about that old crow that calls herself a cook?"

Christina silently promised herself she was going to make this man pay for every evil thing he'd said and done to the Saddler family.

Looking over her shoulder at him, she said, "If you mean Hattie, she's retired for the night."

He grunted. "What about Geraldine and Lex?"

"I—I don't know. This is a big house."

After mouthing a few curse words, he waved the gun toward the swinging door that led from the kitchen to the rest of the house. "I'll take care of them if I have to. Where's the safe in this dump, anyway? In Paul's office?"

"Why would Paul still have an office? He's been dead for twelve years. Thanks to you," she said coldly. "The safe where Geraldine locked the evidence is in the den."

Actually, the only safe in the house that Christina was aware of was located in the den. And she only knew about that one because Lex had opened it one night to show her a set of antique jewelry that had belonged to his great-grandmother.

"Take me to it! And be quick about it!"

He shoved the gun against the back of her rib cage in an effort to hurry her along. Christina shouldered through the swinging doors, then made a sharp right down the dimly lit hallway leading to the den. Normally, the room was the least used in the house. Mostly, Geraldine stuck to her office in the parlor, and Lex used the kitchen for his hangout. As for Christina, she spent most of her time in her little office, but this evening she'd taken her work with her to the den so she could relax on the couch while she waited for Lex to return. Now she took hope in the fact that the den was located at the rear of the house.

If she could throw something through the picture window that faced the back lawn, there was a slight chance one of the men at the bunkhouse would hear the crash and come to investigate.

"You're making a mistake, Lawrence," she said in a deliberately calm tone. "This isn't the way to handle things."

"You said I was stupid, but you and that bitch Geraldine are the stupid ones for thinking I'd give you a cent," he gritted between clenched teeth.

She'd been stupid, all right, Christina thought, for not anticipating this deranged man making a counter move of some sort. But not in a million years would she have thought he would be crazy enough to show up here at the ranch. Damn it! If only she had her revolver. But it was stashed away in the bureau in her bedroom.

When they reached the den, she could see the room

appeared the same as when she'd left it. A table lamp shed a small oval of light near the end of the couch where she'd been working. Nearby, on a small table, a fat scented candle flickered in the semidarkness. Next to it, she'd dropped the folder jammed with notes concerning Paul's case when she'd hurried out to meet Lex. Across the room on the television screen, a female news anchor was continuing to read the evening news and the wild thought that her homicide might be the next story flashed through Christina's mind. But just as quickly, she flung the thought aside.

She had to fight in every way she could against this man. She had to stay alive—to stay with Lex as long as she could, in any way she could.

Deliberately drifting toward the table where the papers were lying, she pointed to the farthest wall of the room. "The safe is over there. Behind that shelving with the horse sculptures."

Following close on her heels, he said, "Get over there and open it! And don't try anything funny!"

"I wouldn't dream of it," Christina said sarcastically. "I'm not a funny kind of girl."

"Shut up and do as I say!"

Intensely aware of the gun pointed at her back, she walked ever so slowly across the room. All the while, her mind was racing, calculating. The only things she recalled being inside the safe were the jewels and a few old maps of the ranch from when Lex's great-grandparents had first purchased the property. There was nothing that she could use to fake Lawrence out, even for a few seconds.

Stall, Christina! Stall! Lex will surely be home soon!

The moment she reached the table, she paused and glanced back at her captor. His gaze was roaming wildly about the room, as though he expected someone to jump out of the shadows. For a second, while his eyes darted away from her, she considered leaping straight at him, but before she could make a move, his eyes were back on her, demonic and threatening.

"Did I tell you to stop, bitch?"

"No. But I don't have the combination to the safe. Besides, all the evidence isn't here. Geraldine has some of it with her."

"Then you'd better get it here. Fast!"

Christina stared at him. If he was brazen enough to walk into the house without knowing how many people might be inside, then he'd obviously come here prepared to shoot whoever got in his way.

"She isn't here. She's away—on a trip with her daughter."

"You're lying! She was supposed to meet me tomorrow at the Red Road Inn. She couldn't be away on a trip."

Seeing she'd obviously confused him, she pressed her luck even further in hopes that she'd get him so distracted, he'd lose his focus. "I don't know where you got the idea that I would allow Geraldine to join our meeting," she told him. "The only guests at that little party were going to be you and me, buster."

His face turned beet-red; then he sucked in a deep breath and shook like a wet dog. Christina braced herself, half expecting him to lift the pistol and fire at her. Instead, he surprised her by suddenly taking on an eerily calm appearance.

"I'm beginning to see right through you," he said, with smug certainty. "You and Geraldine don't have any evidence at all. You're running a bluff. You can't prove anything."

Even as he spoke, Christina's mind was racing ahead, planning her next move. "That's where you're wrong. Geraldine has a tape recording that Paul made a week before you killed him. We discovered it among his things only a few days ago. He was having a very enlightening discussion with Edie Milton."

His beady eyes widened, telling her that she'd momentarily stunned him.

"Edie? She didn't know anything about Paul's little accident."

"Maybe not, but she knew you were a major thief. That's why you disabled the brakes on her car so that she'd be killed on the interstate."

He sneered. "She was greedy—like you. That's why I killed her. She wanted more hush money. But I know she wouldn't have talked about the stock thing. She didn't want to go to the penitentiary any more than I did."

"She did talk," Christina flung back at him. "And so did the person who got the succinylcholine for you. Geraldine has a signed confession."

His mouth fell wide open. "Gloria Westmore? How—she moved out of the state! You couldn't have known about her!"

Suddenly, from somewhere inside the house, the sound of a door opening and closing caught Lawrence's attention, and his gaze swung toward the open doorway.

Christina realized it was her one opportunity to make a move. All at once, she snatched up the burning candle and leaped to one side, out of the path of the gun barrel.

From the corner of her eye, she could see him turning, aiming and preparing to shoot. At the same time, she ducked and flung the candle straight at the picture window. The heavy metal holder crashed through the glass, while the burning wax stuck to the lace curtains, sending small flames crawling up the fabric.

"Christina!"

Lex's yell sounded somewhere in the hallway and she tried to shout a warning back at him, but the sound of her voice was blocked out as Lawrence fired the pistol at her.

Wildly, she dove behind an armchair while across the room the flames were growing, filling the room with smoke. She could hear bullets sinking into the padded upholstery as Lawrence began firing the gun into the chair. At that moment, Christina wondered if she'd ever see Lex again.

When Lex shot into the room, he hardly noticed the fire consuming the curtains and spreading across the outside wall. Through the smoke, he could see Lawrence, the gun raised in his hand as he moved straight at Christina.

Fear and rage poured through Lex, blinding him to everything except saving the woman he loved. Like a rampaging bull, he charged across the room and, with a flying leap, tackled the man from behind.

When both men hit the floor, the impact was so great that Lawrence lost his grip on the pistol and the weapon went sliding across the tile. Lex immediately rolled Lawrence on his back, with plans to smash his fist into the other man's face, but he was already knocked unconscious and was as limp as a rag.

Seeing the man was no longer a threat, Lex rose to his feet and shouted, "Christina! Where are you?"

Sobbing with relief, she emerged from behind the chair and stumbled straight into his arms.

"Oh, Lex, thank God you finally got here!"

"Christina! Oh, Christina!" His hands raced wildly over her face and down her arms as he tried to reassure himself that she was alive and safe. "Are you okay? The bullets didn't hit you?"

"I'm fine—you came just in time!" She glanced down at Lawrence. "We'd better get him and get out of here. This room is about to go up in flames!"

Nodding, Lex quickly leaned down and grabbed Lawrence by the front of his shirt, while nearby Christina scooped up the pistol to use as evidence later.

"Some folks would find it easy to leave him here to burn," Lex muttered as he began to lug the man toward the door. "But, damn it, I can't!"

Christina reached to help him drag the man's deadweight, and as her gaze met his, love flooded her heart. There was no point in denying it anymore.

For more than a century, the Saddler house had endured storms, lightning strikes and grass fires. With the ranch miles away from any sort of fire department, barns and sheds had often burned to the ground, but the house—the ranch's very heart—had always remained like a proud, invincible fort.

Lex, Matt and several cowboys from the bunkhouse desperately fought the flames with garden hoses and saddle blankets. Miraculously, they managed to contain the fire until a fire truck arrived and doused it completely. But not before the flames had eaten through the outer wall of the den and onto the vine-covered patio.

Later, after the sheriff had carted Lawrence away in handcuffs and the commotion around the house began to settle down, Christina and Lex stood staring at the charred ruins. The sight of his beloved home so scorched and scarred filled her with regret, and she dropped her head onto his shoulder and began to sob.

"I'm so sorry about the house, Lex! I caused the fire

with the candle. But I had to do something—he was going to kill me."

Groaning, he let his arms circle around her, and as he held her tightly against him, he buried his face in her thick curls. "It doesn't matter, darling. Even if the whole thing had burned, it wouldn't have mattered. As long as you're safe."

Lifting her face up to his, she tried to smile through her tears. "Thank you for saving my life," she whispered.

"No thanks necessary," he murmured.

He was bringing his lips down on hers when Matt rounded the corner of the house and cleared his throat loudly.

"Uh—Lex? Sorry to interrupt. But Ripp is waiting out front to take you and Christina to the sheriff's department. Sheriff Travers is waiting to speak with you."

Lex glanced regretfully at Christina. "We'll take this matter up later," he whispered in her ear.

Hours later, just before the sun was beginning to break through the branches of the crepe myrtles surrounding the sheriff's office in Goliad, Christina and Lex finally left the building and headed back to the Sandbur.

The night had been long and weary, but neither one of them had really noticed or complained. Lawrence had been booked on several charges and was finally behind bars, where he belonged. Christina and Lex had spent the past couple of hours giving information to law officials. However, this was only the beginning of the testimonies they'd need to give. Due to the multicounty crimes involved in the case, the Texas Rangers had been called in to deal with the investigation. This afternoon, after Christina and Lex had a chance to rest, they'd be supplying depositions, along with Paul's journal, to the Rangers.

"I just don't get it," Lex said to Christina as he turned the truck onto the main highway that would take them to the Sandbur. "Why did Lawrence show up at the ranch instead of waiting to meet you at the restaurant? He was taking a hell of a chance at being caught."

Christina crossed her legs to get more comfortable, and as she did, she noticed that soot stains from the fire smeared down the front of her jeans. When she'd thrown the candle at the window, some of the hot wax had fallen onto the back of her hand. Blisters had now risen on her skin, but the minor injury couldn't begin to dim the satisfaction she'd felt when they'd watched a deputy escort Lawrence to a jail cell. She'd not captured him exactly the way she'd planned, but he was now where he belonged, and he'd live the rest of his life behind bars. She had no doubt about that.

"Because he didn't have the money to obtain the evidence from us. So he figured he was going to have to get it the only way he knew how—by force. I should have suspected as much, but I was expecting him to show up at the Red Road Inn with a stalling story, which would have been enough on its own to incriminate him."

"Don't feel badly. None of us were thinking Lawrence had enough guts to show his face on the Sandbur. But we should have been considering his sanity rather than his guts," he said, then glanced thoughtfully over at her. "There is something else you can explain to me, though. How did you guess that Lawrence had administered succinylcholine to Dad? That's not an everyday, common compound that normal folks are familiar with."

"After I read the autopsy report on your father, the fact that he had no cuts or contusions kept haunting me. From photos and the information Geraldine had given me, it was obvious that your father was a strong, strapping guy. Over six feet tall and well muscled. Lawrence wouldn't have physically been able to toss him over the side of the boat, and even if he'd tried, the scuffle would have caused some minor injuries, not to mention alerted the other two men that something was happening. Without any outward signs of struggle on Paul's body, it stood to reason that he'd been disabled in some other way."

Lex nodded. "I see the deduction. But the succinylcholine—how did you come up with that particular drug?"

"Lawrence worked as a chemist for Coastal Oil. True, that's different than working in medicine, but he still had a good idea of how chemicals and compounds worked. When he decided to kill your father, I calculated that he'd probably looked for a drug that would be hard to trace, but possible to get his hands on without throwing up too many red flags. Yet in the end, Lex, I guess you could say that I simply made a lucky guess."

His profile grim, Lex shook his head. "Now that Lawrence is talking his head off to try and save his hide, we know that he had a nursing friend that worked in surgery. Apparently, he'd given her a pretty penny to steal a bottle of the stuff from the hospital pharmacy. He'd given her some cock-and-bull story about his wife needing it to relax a bad back, and she'd bought the excuse."

"Her name was Gloria Westmore. I tricked him into letting her name slip while he was holding me at gunpoint in the den," Christina said.

He cast her a wan smile. "You're smart. You know that?"

"I try to be," she said, smiling back at him. But was she really? Christina asked herself. Maybe she was clever about solving crimes and finding people that didn't want to be found.

But had she been smart to fall in love with Lex? Her heart kept singing yes, but her mind continued to worry and wonder.

Just before they'd entered the jail, they'd had a couple of minutes alone together, and Lex had used the time to hold her close and kiss her briefly on the lips. He'd told her how terrified he'd been when Gracia had told him about seeing Lawrence and how relieved he'd been when she'd stumbled out from behind the armchair. Yet he'd not said anything about loving her or about what the future might hold for their relationship. But then, maybe expecting that the trauma of the night might have made him open his heart to love was taking hope a bit too far.

She was lost in her thoughts when he said, "There's still one more thing that I'm curious about, Christina. Red and Harve, how did you know they were innocent in all of this? All the evidence made it appear that they were probably just as guilty as Lawrence in the stock scheme and Dad's death. I believed they were."

Realizing it was important for him to understand what had happened all those years ago when his father died, she answered, "Red and Harve couldn't fake the emotion they showed when they spoke to me about Paul's death. Even after all this time, it shook them to recount the story about their late friend. Both of them said they were so frightened when your dad went overboard that they panicked and ended up making stupid decisions about where to take him for medical help. As for the stock scheme, they simply believed that Lawrence had given them a smart tip, and they'd always been grateful to him for giving them the chance to make a pot of money. Neither man had any clue that Lawrence had stolen private company information and used it to his own advantage."

With a disbelieving shake of his head, Lex said, "What's so incredible to me, Christina, is that Dad went out of his way to be a friend to Lawrence. How could he have turned on him?"

She reached across the console between them and touched her hand to his. "Greed overtakes a lot of people, Lex. But Lawrence is going to pay for his greed now. And in the end, that's what matters the most."

"Yeah," he said softly. "You were so right that first evening you came to the Sandbur, when you spoke to me about finding the truth. It is more important than I could have ever imagined."

By now they had reached the ranch house and Lex parked the truck at the side of the structure, next to Christina's vehicle. Gray daylight was spreading across the yard, and behind them she could hear the guys from the bunkhouse heading down to the barns. The realization suddenly hit Christina that this place had truly become her home. She couldn't picture herself going back to the city and not waking up to Cook's breakfasts, to Lex sitting across the table from her, or to riding across the range with him at her side, eating off a chuck wagon and listening to music around a campfire. Yet now that Paul's case was wrapped up, she had no right or reason to stay here, and that fact was settling in the bottom of her heart like a heavy chunk of ice.

"Finally. We're home and alone," Lex said. Then, with a weary but happy grin, he reached over and pulled her toward him. "And I have about a thousand things I want to say to you."

Home. Could he possibly know how wonderful that sounded to her? The soft look in his eyes sparked a bit of hope in Christina, and she studied his face closely as he drew his head down to hers.

"A thousand?" she whispered. "That's…quite a bit of talking."

"I thought talk was what you wanted."

Hearing him say that he loved her had once seemed so important. But after last night, after going through moments when she'd not known whether she'd remain alive to say anything to Lex, she realized that words weren't always the solution. And right now Christina felt it was more important to show him that she trusted him and how very much she wanted him in her life.

"I've had time to think about that, Lex," she murmured, then reached beneath his arm and pulled the latch on the door. "And we—uh—need to go inside. I want to—show you something important."

His brows peaked with interest, but he didn't ask questions as he climbed to the ground, then helped her out of the cab.

As they walked to the house, she wrapped her hand around his and didn't let go even after they were inside.

The kitchen smelled like fresh coffee, telling her that Cook was already in, but not anywhere to be seen in the room. As much as Christina loved the other woman, she was glad she wasn't around. Christina didn't want anything or anyone to interfere with her plans.

"Where are we going?" he asked as she led him out of the room, down the hall and on toward the staircase. "Don't you want breakfast?"

"We can eat later. This is too important," she told him in a hushed voice.

"There's no reason for being so quiet," he reminded her as they reached the second floor. "Mom is still with Nicci, and they won't be home until later this evening. We're not going to disturb anyone."

"That's right," she told him with a wicked smile, then opened the door to her bedroom and tugged him inside.

After she carefully shut the door behind her, she turned to him and saw a puzzled, almost comical look on his face.

"Christina, what are you doing?"

Smiling seductively, she said, "I thought you were an experienced man, Lex Saddler. Do I have to spell this out to you? I want us to make love. And you told me if that ever happened again, I'd have to do the asking."

The confused look in his eyes suddenly turned somber, and she began to tremble as he cupped his hands around the sides of her face.

"Why now, Christina?"

Regret filled her eyes. "Last night, when Lawrence started firing his gun, I was terrified he might kill you or me and that I—I'd never have the chance to tell you how much I love you."

His eyes full of wonder, he cupped his hands against the sides of her face. "You love me? Oh, Christina! Why didn't you tell me before?"

Why hadn't she? Now that both of them had been in serious danger of losing their lives, her reasons seemed ridiculous. "I didn't think it would matter to you. You'd said that other women had fallen in love with you and they'd not gotten any love from you in return—I thought I'd be just one more."

The soft glimmer she saw in his eyes looked incredibly like love, and the idea set her heart pounding loudly in her ears.

"Oh, darling, you're not just any woman. You're my life!" Bending his head, he brought his lips next to hers. "The night we found the disk with Dad's journal, I realized I loved you, but I couldn't tell you. I knew the words would be just that—words to you and nothing more. And then last night—when I saw Lawrence about to shoot you, I was seeing my world ending right before my eyes. Christina, weeks, months, years wouldn't make me love you any more than I do now. I want you to be my wife. You've got to believe me."

Incredible joy swept through her, and she stared at him in amazement. "Your wife? I never thought I'd hear you say those words."

"Well, I'm waiting to hear your answer. I'm waiting to hear you say you can be happy living here on the Sandbur, with me."

She blinked rapidly as happy tears filled her eyes. "I love the ranch, Lex. I was just wondering how I was ever going to be able to leave it—and you. Now I won't have to. I've been a career woman for over ten years, and it's been good. I want to be a wife and mother now—more than anything."

Laughing now, he lifted her off her feet, then allowed the front of her body to slide against his until the tips of her toes were back on the floor and her lips were hovering beneath his.

"Dad has been gone for nearly twelve years," he said gently. "When you first came to the ranch, I never believed that you—that the two of us together—would ever discover what really happened to him."

"But we did," she whispered happily.

"Yeah, we did. But more than that, Christina, you walked into my heart and showed me what it's like to love. Really love. And, honey, I may not be the ideal husband or the greatest dad, but I'm damn well going to try."

"That's all I'll ever ask, my love," she whispered, then with a happy sigh, closed the last breath of space between their lips.

Epilogue

Six weeks later, on a hot September evening, the wedding guests finally vacated the backyard at the Saddler house. The band had carried away the last of their instruments, and now all that was left behind of Lex and Christina's reception was a few family members, the mess and plenty of fond memories.

Weary, but very contented, Geraldine wandered through the empty tables piled high with leftover food, dirty plates and champagne glasses. She'd just seen her last child married, and though she expected some mothers would be feeling a bit melancholy, she wasn't. Her prayers had finally been answered. Lex had found and married the love of his life.

Pausing at the end of one of the tables, she looked toward the arbor, where Nicci and Mercedes were sitting in lawn chairs, visiting with their cousins. It hadn't taken long for carpenters to repair the fire damage to the house, but it would take the honeysuckle much longer to grow back, and she hated that.

"Looks as bare as a newborn's butt, don't it?"

Geraldine looked toward the voice to see Cook sitting alone beneath the branch of a live oak. The older woman was all dressed up in red silk and black high heels, and her long hair was wound in an elaborate chignon at the back of her head. In spite of her age, she still looked beautiful, and earlier this evening Geraldine had had to fight back sentimental tears as she'd watched her son dance Cook around the dance floor.

"Yes, it's bare," Geraldine replied. "But it will grow back."

She walked over to where Cook sat on a wrought-iron bench and sank down next to her.

"Why are you sitting here alone? Are you feeling okay?"

Cook snorted. "Course, I am."

"You're not fretting about all this mess, are you? I've hired extra workers to take care of all this, and remember, you have Caroline to help you now."

Gabe's childhood friend had finally managed to make the move down here to the ranch from Oklahoma City. So far, she was working out well, and Cook had already grown fond of the woman and her young son.

Cook waved a hand through the air. "I'm not worried."

Geraldine sighed. "It was a lovely wedding. Christina looked gorgeous. They should have a nice honeymoon on Padre Island. The Morgans are letting them stay at their private beach house. They'll have the place to themselves for a whole week."

"Mmm. It was a beautiful wedding," Cook agreed. "And I was glad Christina's parents managed to attend. Her mother came off as a bit of a floozy, but she seemed happy for Christina. Guess that's the important thing. I liked her dad. He was quiet, but in a nice way."

Geraldine smiled wistfully. "I'm glad Retha and Delbert

were able to attend this special event in their daughter's life. I only wish Christina could find her brother. I got the feeling that she was thinking especially about him today."

"Well, sure," Cook agreed. "She'd like to have her brother back."

"Oh. Speaking of finding people," Geraldine said. "Did you hear that Ripp and Mac have started searching for their missing mother? They've gotten a clue as to her whereabouts, and they've decided they need to find out what really happened with her. The same way I needed to know about Paul."

"Everybody needs family," Cook murmured sagely.

Both women went quiet after that; then suddenly Cook bent her head and pressed a handkerchief to her eyes. Rattled by the sight, Geraldine laid a comforting hand on the woman's shoulder.

"Why, Hattie, are you crying?"

She sniffed. "I can't help it. Lex has always been my little boy, too."

Smiling now, Geraldine patted her back. "He's not going anywhere, Hattie. He'll be living right here like he always has. And think of it this way. We'll have babies in the house again."

Lifting her head, Cook dabbed away her tears and chuckled. "That's right. And knowing Lex, it won't take him long to get them here."

* * * * *

The Saddlers are settled, but what will Ripp and Mac discover when they seek out their mother?
Find out in A TEXAN ON HER DOORSTEP,
coming in March 2009.

Celebrate 60 years of pure reading pleasure with Harlequin® Books!

Harlequin Romance® is celebrating by showering you with DIAMOND BRIDES *in February 2009. Six stories that promise to bring a touch of sparkle to your life, with diamond proposals and dazzling weddings, sparkling brides and gorgeous grooms!*

Enjoy a sneak peek at Caroline Anderson's TWO LITTLE MIRACLES, available February 2009 from Harlequin Romance®

"I'VE FOUND HER."

Max froze.

It was what he'd been waiting for since June, but now—now he was almost afraid to voice the question. His heart stalling, he leaned slowly back in his chair and scoured the investigator's face for clues. "Where?" he asked, and his voice sounded rough and unused, like a rusty hinge.

"In Suffolk. She's living in a cottage."

Living. His heart crashed back to life, and he sucked in a long, slow breath. All these months he'd feared—

"Is she well?"

"Yes, she's well."

He had to force himself to ask the next question. "Alone?"

The man paused. "No. The cottage belongs to a man called John Blake. He's working away at the moment, but he comes and goes."

God. He felt sick. So sick he hardly registered the next few words, but then gradually they sank in. "She's got *what?*"

"Babies. Twin girls. They're eight months old."

"Eight—" he echoed under his breath. "They must be his."

He was thinking out loud, but the P.I. heard and corrected him.

"Apparently not. I gather they're hers. She's been there since mid-January last year, and they were born during the summer—June, the woman in the post office thought. She was more than helpful. I think there's been a certain amount of speculation about their relationship."

He'd just bet there had. God, he was going to kill her. Or Blake. Maybe both of them.

"Of course, looking at the dates, she was presumably pregnant when she left you, so they could be yours, or she could have been having an affair with this Blake character before..."

He glared at the unfortunate P.I. "Just stick to your job. I can do the math," he snapped, swallowing the unpalatable possibility that she'd been unfaithful to him before she'd left. "Where is she? I want the address."

"It's all in here," the man said, sliding a large envelope across the desk to him. "With my invoice."

"I'll get it seen to. Thank you."

"If there's anything else you need, Mr. Gallagher, any further information—"

"I'll be in touch."

"The woman in the post office told me Blake was away at the moment, if that helps," he added quietly, and opened the door.

Max stared down at the envelope, hardly daring to open it, but when the door clicked softly shut behind the P.I., he eased up the flap, tipped it and felt his breath jam in his throat as the photos spilled out over the desk.

Oh, lord, she looked gorgeous. Different, though. It took him a moment to recognize her, because she'd grown her hair, and it was tied back in a ponytail, making her look younger and somehow freer. The blond highlights were gone, and it was back to its natural soft golden-brown, with a little curl in the end of the ponytail that he wanted to thread his finger through and tug, just gently, to draw her back to him.

Crazy. She'd put on a little weight, but it suited her. She looked well and happy and beautiful, but oddly, considering how desperate he'd been for news of her for the past year—one year, three weeks and two days, to be exact—it wasn't only Julia who held his attention after the initial shock. It was the babies sitting side by side in a supermarket trolley. Two identical and absolutely beautiful little girls.

* * * * *

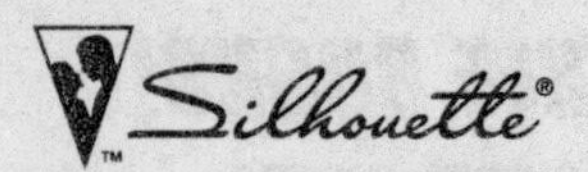

SPECIAL EDITION®

COMING NEXT MONTH

#1951 VALENTINE'S FORTUNE—Allison Leigh
Fortunes of Texas: Return to Red Rock
Rescuing the pregnant damsel in distress was all in a day's work for firefighter Darr Fortune. But when he was stranded with sexy, mysterious "Barbara Burton" during a freak Valentine's Day snowstorm, he looked forward to uncovering all her secrets....

#1952 ALWAYS VALENTINE'S DAY—Kristin Hardy
Holiday Hearts
Things were about to get very steamy on this Alaskan cruise, as party girl Larkin Hayes crossed paths with lobbyist-turned-Vermont-dairy-farmer Christopher Trask. Could this unlikely duo make some Valentine's Day magic to last a lifetime?

#1953 THE NANNY SOLUTION—Teresa Hill
Self-made millionaire Simon Collier needed a nanny—for his out-of-control pooch! Audrey Graham fit the bill...and then some. Not only did Simon's five-year-old daughter warm immediately to Audrey, but the live-in dogsitter soon soothed the savage beast of the single dad's lonely heart, too.

#1954 THE TEXAN'S TENNESSEE ROMANCE—Gina Wilkins
After losing her job, attorney Natalie Lofton retreated to her family's Smoky Mountain cabin to nurse her wounds. Then she met handyman Casey Walker. He wasn't very handy—truth be told, Casey was a Dallas lawyer on leave—but he *was* about to prove he could mend hearts with the best of them.

#1955 THEIR SECOND-CHANCE CHILD—Karen Sandler
Fostering Family
Tony Herrara must have been crazy to hire his ex-wife Rebecca Tipton to oversee his vocational bakery and café for adult foster kids! But Becca was best for the job...and his four-year-old daughter fell for Becca instantly. Were Tony and Becca headed down the road to renewed heartache, or was this the second chance they never dreamed possible?

#1956 THE MOMMY MAKEOVER—Kristi Gold
When the little girl bought her widowed mom personal training sessions, sexy health club owner Kieran O'Brien was charmed. Erica Stevens—the mom in question—wasn't. But as Erica warmed to the routine, she discovered that the muscle getting the real workout was her heart—which beat faster whenever Kieran was around....

SSECNMBPA0109